Divine Hiddenness

Divine Hiddenness
Parables on Why God Hides Himself

Nathan Glover
"The Plagiarist"

Illustrated by Tessa Sentell

XULON PRESS

Xulon Press
555 Winderley Pl, Suite 225
Maitland, FL 32751
407.339.4217
www.xulonpress.com

© 2024 by Nathan Glover
Revised 2025

Illustrated by Tessa Sentell

All rights reserved solely by the author. The author guarantees all contents are original and do not infringe upon the legal rights of any other person or work. No part of this book may be reproduced in any form without the permission of the author.

Due to the changing nature of the Internet, if there are any web addresses, links, or URLs included in this manuscript, these may have been altered and may no longer be accessible. The views and opinions shared in this book belong solely to the author and do not necessarily reflect those of the publisher. The publisher therefore disclaims responsibility for the views or opinions expressed within the work.

Unless otherwise indicated, Scripture quotations taken from the Holy Bible, New International Version (NIV). Copyright © 1973, 1978, 1984, 2011 by Biblica, Inc.™. Used by permission. All rights reserved.

Scripture quotations taken from the English Standard Version (ESV). Copyright © 2001 by Crossway, a publishing ministry of Good News Publishers. Used by permission. All rights reserved.

Paperback ISBN-13: 978-1-66289-782-5
eBook ISBN-13: 978-1-66289-783-2

To my children.

Special thanks to Brad Lebakken for having breakfast with me out of the blue and gifting me a contract with Xulon so that I could publish this book for free.

"These lively, memorable vignettes *show*, rather than merely tell, an all-important but oft-overlooked truth: that a God who perfectly loves human beings would relate to us in a way that would form us to be, not mere acquiescent spectators of his power, but mature persons who trust deeply, marvel at creation, and, above all, imitate his self-sacrificial love. A moving picture of the heart of God and the point of human life!"

— *Griffin Klemick*,
Department of Philosophy, Hope College

"Why isn't God more obvious? If he loves us and wants us to believe in him, why does he often seem hidden? This is one of the deepest and most common questions people ask about God. Rather than attempting to resolve this issue with a logical syllogism, Nathan Glover explores it using an engaging narrative style. His stories give fresh perspective and enhance our imagination about what it means to pursue real relationship. He also demonstrates why some of our simplistic demands would backfire, and helps us see that God may not be as hidden as he seems."

— *Matthew Mittelberg*,
Director of Content and Speaker for Apologetics, Inc.

"Reading this book is like experiencing a fever dream during a university lecture. And yet, it inspires a revived sense of awe and admiration for questions asked- much like the dreamer who awakes to the smell of strong coffee."

– *Thomas Barry*,
Founder of Small Media Large

"In this beautifully crafted collection of vignettes, Nathan Glover skillfully weaves together humour and imagination to draw out insights about the nature of the human condition and the perennial question of why God isn't more obvious in the world. Skillfully ranging over various genres - be it fantasy, fictional autobiography, historical fiction - Glover finds numerous angles from which to shed light on these age-old puzzles. For anyone who has ever pondered these topics, this is a must read."

– *Max Baker-Hytch*,
Wycliffe Hall, Oxford University

Table of Contents

	Page
Preface—A Very Optional Read	xv
Chapter One The Orator	1
Chapter Two—The Helicopter Parent	13
Chapter Three—The Visionary	21
Chapter Four—Growing Up	35
Chapter Five—Grandfather	41
Chapter Six—The Rules of War and Boundaries of Love	47
Chapter Seven—Paul and Luke	69
Afterword	85

All illustrations created by Tessa Sentel.
tessakaycreative@gmail.com
@tkacreative

There is a great host of people I must thank for the creation of this book. My wife has sacrificed my company on countless occasions. She has watched the kids so many times when I was out writing. She has also read and edited most of this book. Thus, it is no exaggeration to say that the book would not exist without her. Beyond her, there are several other people who deserve hearty thanks. The most influential of these is my good friend RY Kopf. So many hours my friend, so many late nights. I hope you feel as I do, that there is no one else I would have rather started this with. In addition to RY are Roseanna Lee, Laura Anderson, Griffin Klemick, Abby and Doug Graham, Hannah Holtzinger and my mother. All these people read and re-read my book and have offered fantastic advice on how to improve it. I also must thank Thomas Barry and the men that meet at his house on Tuesday nights for their help with the project. Beyond that I have my amazing artist, Tessa Kay Sentell. As you, the reader no doubt see, she has done an amazing job leading your imagination into each of these stories. I must also acknowledge my mentors from the grave C.S. Lewis and G.K. Chesterton. Their fingerprints are all over this work. In the final essay written by a fictional fusion of the two authors, there are some very near

Divine Hiddenness

quotations that I obviously cannot attribute to them in the text but will acknowledge them here. But most of all I need to thank the Creator. For this book is nothing more than His wisdom, as I have strained to see it through dust in a mirror.

Preface

A Very Optional Read

There are two types of people who will read this book. The type that should read this preface before proceeding and the type that should not. The type that, "should not" can be described succinctly as adventurers. You are a person who does not want signposts. Your imagination simply needs something to chew on and you will do the rest. Ideas are like friends to you, and you are as comfortable among them as a lion tamer is among lions. You do not watch movie trailers. You are scared to watch teasers. You do not read spoilers. You want to be surprised and you want to be taken on a journey. If these things describe you, stop reading and go to chapter one.

Hello everyone else, my roadmap crew. I have written this for you. Below are your trailers and some spoilers. Below, I will explain what I intend to do in this book. I will then explain how each chapter works towards the book's goal.

The goal of the book is to provide a pictorial explanation of why God hides himself from our conscious experience. This more than any question has plagued me, and the following pictures have aided me not only in understanding God but worshiping Him. I want to be clear, I offer pictures, not proofs. You will not find theological syllogisms demonstrating that God is justified when He withholds His power. What you will find are pictures, based on Christian doctrines, that may aid a person in understanding why God restrains Himself. In the following paragraphs I will provide a trailer for each chapter telling you some (not all) of what you will find there and how these chapters may help you understand God's hiddenness better.

Chapter 1

The first thing to note about this chapter is that it is a farce. Laugh a little. If you find it sort of silly, that is because it is silly. But it was written to demonstrate how humans might have responded to God revealing Himself like a sort of movie star. A red-carpet entrance if you will. In this story God is extremely visible and obvious but also still distant enough to allow some autonomy and free-will. In this hypothetical, God does allow for some human purposes and responsibility, but has made His existence, plans and purposes more obvious.

Chapter 2

This chapter was written to show how suffocating God could have made our existence. In this hypothetical, everything about God is extremely obvious and all human behavior is micromanaged so as to avoid all evil or even opportunity for evil of any kind. Some autonomy is left to the female main character, but that autonomy is highly restricted within the guard rails of omniscient optimization. Here God feigns giving the girl purpose; but in order to keep her reality perfect God never leaves anything to chance. The girl's reality is subject to God's perpetual micromanagement so that nothing short of perfection can result. Thus, God essentially resorbs any purpose or autonomy He pretends to give the girl. Though she has her own feelings, thoughts and conscious experiences, for all intents and purposes there is no place where God ends, and she begins. Humanity as pet goldfish is right on the nose.

Chapter 3

This chapter was written to show how God might have created a sort of pleasure world. In this hypothetical, God places someone in an area where the person can experience all sorts of pleasures without any pains. Here, the world isn't so much suffocating as it is disorienting. The person cannot appreciate pleasure because he has become numb to it through repetition. Equally, he cannot appreciate his experience because he has no backdrop of hardship or difficulty to aid him in evaluating the worth of what he is seeing, tasting, enjoying etc. He does not feel suffocated by God because there is no feigned giving of purpose, meaning, or autonomy to him. In this world he is bored. In this world he cannot grow. In this world he is perfectly safe, perfectly docile, and perfectly stupid. He has the ability to experience new things but no ability to engage with and thus deeply enjoy any of those things.

Chapter 4

Here, the book transitions from possible worlds where God may have done things differently, to the wisdom of His actions in the world He has designed. In chapter 4 we learn about a boy who discovers that the way to appreciate anything is to give yourself to something. He learns that until he does something, he cannot understand, much less enjoy that thing.

Chapter 5

In this chapter we see how the reality of the family, and the causality necessarily associated with creating families, generates compounding momentum with concern to human choices. In other words, necessarily, the choices made by earlier generations will affect the subsequent generations. Additionally, choices made by some generations can create impossibilities for future generations.

Chapter 6

This chapter is a series of letters between angels. These angels are asking all sorts of questions with concern to why they and God are not more active with humans and against

Satan and evil. This chapter will connect dots between different theological concepts and common human experiences. Amongst many things, this section explores the Fall, what separation from God really entails, free-will and causality and the necessary connections between all of these things.

This chapter deals with the question of why God would not want to reveal Himself to every individual person in dreams, visions, or short encounters. The answer is a complicated amalgam of consequences from the Fall, the relationship between love, free-will and trust, and some causal necessities associated with human purpose, meaning and dignity. This chapter also provides a framework for understanding why God does, at times, reveal Himself in visions, dreams, and encounters.

This chapter also intends to demonstrate the necessity of God's distance between Himself and man if meaningful human decision making is to be achieved. While also, affirming the mankind's properly ancient intuition that God feels farther away than He ought to be. Chapter 6 explains this ancient sense of estrangement by appealing to the Christian doctrine of the Fall. The argument essentially being that because of human sin we are farther away from God then we ought to be. God has distanced Himself from our conscious experience more than even He would like too. God has done this because humanity through sin has declared God untrustworthy, God is left with no recourse but to distance Himself. If I say, I do not trust God, how can

He prove His trustworthiness? Anything He says or does can also be deemed untrustworthy. God is left then, to allow those that do not trust him to experience the consequences of their ideas through action and either learn from these experiences or become obstinate enemies of God.

Afterword

Here is written a defense of the incarnation of Jesus Christ. In this newspaper article, reasons are given as to why God revealing Himself to humanity as Jesus of Nazareth is the best possible revelation anyone could have imagined.

Chapter One
The Orator

Hello great grandpa Bedford, as the first person ever cryogenically frozen in 1967 you probably can't hear what I'm about to say, but I need to get something off my chest. Anyway, thanks for being here. I've been thinking a lot lately about my time in Oxford. I love to look at the pictures so I can relive falling in love with it. I never lived anywhere else that suited me better. The endless number of people to philosophize with, the countless places designed for just that. People from every country, food from every country, and above all, the bottomless lectures one might consume. I was a part of the Oxford Union. As such, I had access to a hoard of visiting speakers, ranging from Mark Cuban to John Kerry, Al Sharpton to Pamela Anderson, Jordan Peterson to Peter Griffin. Needless to say, a wide variety of celebrities have found in their mailbox an invitation from the Oxford Union. And as was my custom on Friday nights, I was in line to hear from such a celebrity. But not just such a celebrity. On this Friday night, I found myself waiting in line for the most prominent speaker the Oxford Union had ever landed. During the first term of my second year, the speaker was God.

How had they done this, you ask? Well, the story is as astonishing as the reality. One fall afternoon, a shining metallic spaceship landed across from Salisbury Cathedral. The Bishop of Salisbury was in America engaging in a protest and thus, was not in his bishopric when the spacecraft arrived. The ship did not move for 72 hours. News, police, military, you name it, were all at the scene giving the ship round-the-clock attention. Within those 72 hours, it is estimated that over 10 million people had made their way to Salisbury. A great multitude of them were living in tents all around the military perimeter. The migration was so intense that Salisbury's mayor asked the army to reduce the tent city. Unexpectedly, the tensity went up as the tents went down because the tent-dwellers were intent on remaining in tents; that is until a tank accidentally destroyed Salisbury Cathedral. An M1 Abram moved through the crowd to point its barrel at the extraterrestrial vessel and was forced to veer suddenly—for a tank—To narrowly avoid crushing a couple taking a selfie. And with the dread of a man waiting for water to overflow a toilet, the world watched this armored cannon crawl into a 13th century masterpiece and bring it down. Miraculously, no one was killed in the accident – though a few were injured. However, one thing did die: the faith of the bishop, who was quoted afterward saying, "If there were a God, He would have preserved my Cathedral." As one might imagine, some dozens more oddities and injuries took place around this flying machine. But after 72 hours, an administrative voice came from the ship exclaiming, "Hello, I come transporting God, and He has come to speak to you. He will only speak at Oxford University and only as a speaker invited by the Oxford Union. Please send forward a representative from the Oxford Union, with credentials, so that we can negotiate the details."

Within two weeks, hundreds of Oxford and military personnel had approached the ship and negotiated God's appearance at Oxford. There was pandemonium across the planet. It was on every screen, every minute, of every day. And I know what your thinking; how was I one of the people who attended the globally anticipated lecture given by God?

Well Grandpa Bedford, my dream was to attend Oxford University, and when I graduated high school here in America, my dream came true. But none of this explains how I was among the elites attending this event. The answer? Dumb luck. As you can imagine, tickets for this event were priced in the millions of dollars, even for the cheap seats. Seats at the front were purchased by governments for their heads of state, and each seat went for roughly a billion dollars. Jeff Bezos alone was the only non-head of state at the front; he was, reportedly, there to advise the American President. Bezos secured his seat next to the VP by donating a measly 2 billion tax-deductible dollars to the President's next campaign.

This massive influx of money allowed Oxford University to build a stadium for the event. Oxford elected to build the stadium on a section of the vast tracts of land owned by St. John's College. The stadium was not massive, seating only 30,000 people. Oxford argued, since they would need to use the stadium after the event, they would not build something more extensive. This was mocked furiously by Cambridge. Qatar Airways ponied up 20 million pounds for naming rights. Despite the modest size, Qatar Airways Arena was state of the art. Heated cushions, touch screens, desks, cup holders, refrigerators, headsets for translation were all built into the seats. Several Michelin Star restaurants supplied the stadium food. Maccallan was contracted to the tune of millions to provide their unconscionable 100 rare whisky in casks stationed throughout. Magnificent artwork and sculptures lined the walls and walkways. Truly a spectacle. Equally astonishing is that it took a mere month to build. Multiple corporations and governments worked around the clock to create what would be a one million square foot golden dome. At any rate, how did I get there? Well, the Oxford Union was gifted by Oxford University and the UK government ten free tickets among the cheap seats. How were they to distribute the tickets? Well, each member of Oxford University was given the opportunity to

The Orator

pay three hundred pounds and enter a lottery to hear God. As you can imagine, everyone who could find the money entered, including me, and I won. I read the email confirmation a hundred times. Upon the one hundred and first read I began to weep. I wept until my tears short-circuited my keyboard. I called my parents. I made a Tik Tok. I got wasted. I will never forget that day.

So, there I was, standing in a large glass vestibule behind Bill Gates' armed guard waiting to get in. The first-floor atrium was a metropolis of sculptures. I was blown away both by the classical artwork and the modern masterpieces brought in for the event. Given most prominent position was Michaelangelo's "David" and Marcel Duchamp's "Fountain," and across from them, Jeff Koons' "Balloon Dog." After my first escalator ride, I lost Bill and found myself standing with the other winners of the Oxford raffle. We stuck together, filming every second, as we squeezed around people from all over the world surveying the stadium. In the fastest two hours of my life, we saw as much as we could, secured beverages and got to our seats. There were several members of the press all around us in addition to the winners of the U.S.A. raffle. A choir was performing as everyone waited for God. The Pope's choir was singing, and several other religious choirs waited in line. After about the 5th choir, I was done with my drinks and started looking around for my program. After the 11th choir performance, it was announced that God had entered the building. The place was silent as He took the stage. I brought binoculars and was looking through them. He had to be seven feet tall or larger with gigantic muscles. He looked like something out of a comic book. He was, and still is, the most attractive man I have ever seen. When He got to the stage, He was directed to sit down. The God-man complied, and then several heads of state came to the microphone to welcome Him. After the 11th head of state finished speaking, a woman named Ursula from Germany motioned to the God-man; it was finally time.

As He strolled up to the mic, cameras flashed, and videos rolled. Every celebrity was live streaming. Every student was texting. I was trying to take a selfie where you could see God in the picture beside my face, but God was too small to see. I was determined to get a decent shot, and after He had been talking for about 20 minutes, I succeeded. I applied the perfect filter to the perfect picture and uploaded it to my relevant social media platforms. Finally, after making sure my followers were taken care of, I could settle in and listen to this legendary speaker. He talked about how He was a good God. He talked about that a lot. He also talked about how He loved people. It was like, the best political campaign commercial ever, we were all very impressed. I started talking with those seated next to me about how crazy it was that we were here. We all agreed that this was something we would tell our grandkids about one day. Suddenly, the 42 ounces of iced coffee I drank during the choir performances hit me hard. So, I got up to use the restroom. On my way back, I grabbed a duck pizza from Osteria Francescana; the price was ridiculous, but this was probably my only chance to try this restaurant, so I willingly paid for it. When I sat back down, God was wrapping up.

"To all of humanity, know that I care about you. I want you all to have a good time in your lives and be decent and respectable human beings. Never change who you are, but always work on getting better." After God punctuated His final remark with a self-assured wink and finger guns, the crowd erupted. People rose to their feet; thunderous applause rang through the auditorium. Because all my food was on my lap, I couldn't rise to ovate; but I also didn't want to seem disrespectful, so I got up as much as I could and slapped my food container in approval. After that, God raised his hands and began to run down one of the aisles. He disappeared through a set of doors. People began to stop clapping, thinking the show was over. When suddenly, God emerged again, running up a different aisle and then down another one. People clapped again and more vigorously. As God turned to run up a fourth aisle, He raised His hands to give people high fives. He got back on the stage and yelled! "I love you, Oxford!" Some people began to weep. One woman fainted. He went down another aisle, this time doing cartwheels. The paramedics came to remove the fainted woman. In the commotion, the Bishop of Salisbury, who had previously renounced his faith, came up to the mic and said in a loud, triumphant voice, "God has been here!" As armed guards removed the Bishop, God began to fly. God circled around the second level of seating giving high fives to celebrities and then, as if yanked by a chord, shot upward towards the roof and appeared to fly through it. The roof was not damaged, it was a miracle.

The applause continued. Finally, the cheering subsided, and everyone sat down. The President of the United States took the stage and with tears in his eyes said, "This is the most important day in our world's history, and I think we all know what this means for my international platform towards improving global infrastructure, tax reform and commerce. God bless us all." At this, rows of ten-foot champagne bottles appeared behind each section and uncorked foaming goodness all over the crowd. Soaked exultation lifted to the skies. People wept. People embraced. Everything came together. Delegates from North and South Korea shook hands. Pepsi and Coke were mixed. Skittles and M&Ms were bagged together. Someone made donuts filled with baked beans. The world was one! What a day!

It's been a little over three years since I saw God on stage. A few hours after the event, God went back inside His spaceship, gave the peace sign, and flew back into eternity. I was amazed and felt so important. I was one of the mere 30,000 people who got to hear God live. I was interviewed dozens of times, appeared in a few newspapers, appeared on a reality tv show, and wrote my memoirs into a best-seller. Beyond all of that, I have signed a two-year advertising contract with Vitamin Water, and New Balance has issued me a fifty-million-dollar shoe deal. The shoe is called "God-Says." Needless to say, my life has been transformed. I am now an Oxford Graduate with a speaking and advertising career. I am back in the United States and living next to Lebron James. Everything has been amazing. That is, until about two months ago.

Two months ago, I got a little introspective after an unsuccessful date. I couldn't sleep, so I started looking at some of the responses to "the most important day in our world's history." I had read them all before. The news industry adapted to take full advantage of the first televised God-sighting. NBC, ABC, CNN, FOX News, USA Today, New York Times, Washington Post, Washington News: every news agency added a God News component to their coverage. Some had regular front-page articles, others created a God tab on their webpage, and the major stations added an entire department to their newsroom, including investigative journalists. For a little over a year after the event, I spent my nights reading every report and opinion by anyone and everyone who cared to write about God's big speech. By year's end, I was almost sure I had read everything that had been reported in the English language. But on this night, I discovered something I had not yet seen. It was an article by a Catholic man named Clive Gilbert Lewis Keith, who wrote his review a few months after the event for a local newspaper in Kensington London called The Illustrated London News.

Seeing something I had not yet read, I clicked on the article and was floored and delighted to see not just a review, but a lengthy review. So many theological treatises of the event were three-hundred words or less. I was hungry for more content. From almost the moment I started the article, I knew I was reading something different from anything I had read before. For starters, the man's vocabulary was on a different level, and, for finishers, he had the coldest take I had ever read about God. Or at least, that's what I thought at first. I knew he was wrong, and it was infuriating. I sat in my bed and tried to sleep, but my brain would not turn off. I was fuming. I decided to go back and reread it to create a rebuttal media campaign. And it was during the second slower read, that I started to become worried about what this man was saying. I had never heard anyone talk with such irreverence towards God, and thought this especially odd from a person spending his life studying God. Mr. Keith had not been there on the day God arrived, but he had read the transcript of what God said. I will not reproduce the whole paper here, but what Mr. Keith argued was that the one whom the majority of humanity called God was, perhaps too familiar and too different to be who we believed him to be.

One section is worth quoting in its entirety.

"This tall, handsome, polite man introduced to us as the Almighty has said many flattering things about himself and about us. But has he proved them? He has said that he is good. But to whom has he shown His goodness? He has said that he loves us, but what does he mean by this phrase? Some people say they love their families, and others love their food; how is "God" using this word when he says it to us? He comes to us and speaks words we say to each other every day. He recites Facebook posts my niece might have written. He says all the familiar things a television host might repeat about God, and, without another word or action, he sends the world a peace sign and peaces out. What does this man mean?

Some may think that I am joining the small chorus of objectors who are both confused and offended by God's pathetic use of the English language. I am not. Some may think I hate that his style has been embraced at the popular level. On the contrary, it is one of the few things about this deity that I find appealing. Some may think I am frustrated with giant swathes of humanity leaving Christianity in order to follow the 'True God's Religion.' This is regrettable; however, this is not my issue with Him. My problem, lest anyone is confused, is that this 'God' came to humanity speaking of his goodness, speaking of his love, speaking of endless joy and hope for tomorrow. And then he does nothing. I do not deny the existence of goodness, but what assurances do I have that this large man is the source of that goodness? What goodness did he, in the 22 hours that we knew him, display?

In short, what I am arguing is that a man's worth is not dependent on what he says about his moral conduct; it is dependent on His moral conduct. We have heard from 'God' that he is good. But goodness is not in the telling; it is in the doing. In other words, the claim of merit can only be confirmed or denied through history. The God of the Old Testament spoke of His goodness and then did good things among Israel, and then in the New Testament, He did one better. He became an ordinary man and showed men not just that He was good but how they might imitate His goodness. It is the moral life of Jesus that drew men and women to Him. But the 'God' of our age asks for genuinely blind faith."

When I finished reading these words the second time, I became rather worried and a little squeamish. I felt pretty uncomfortable and wanted to go to sleep. But I was too uncomfortable to sleep, so I tried reading articles from more reputable news sources. I checked my monetized platforms and read my top comments. I looked at the views on some of my most recent YouTube videos. Finally, I fell asleep. And that's it, that's the story grandpa, that's the story. On the surface nothing has changed. But inside, I have not felt the same since I read that article. I find myself questioning things, especially considering how the world has changed since then.

Chapter Two
The Helicopter Parent

Hi, I'm Chloe, I'm 16, and I am trying not to hate my parents. So, I already know what you're going to say: "Why is a privileged, white, upper-class girl like you complaining about her perfect life?" And, look: I get it. I have everything. My mother is a partner at her law firm. My father wrote the Konami code or whatever, so we are literally billionaires. My dad collects like, literally everything and he is eccentric about it. His fish collection is literally a giant glass tube that runs throughout our nine-story house in Nevada. Literally, hundreds of fish displayed in every room. And like my dad's fish I have everything I could ever need or want. I have more than one car, more than one house, and a six-figure allowance. So yeah, I know I will not get a lot of sympathy, but I absolutely NEED to write this, or I will go insane.

So, what is my deal? Well, it's really not that hard to get: my parents control everything. Like totally oppressive. Like I don't actually have a life. I know you're like, "so, what?" But you don't get it. Okay, so, example: I'm walking to my friend's house because we're going to hang out with some boys at her rooftop pool. I know, it sounds like everything's perfect, but wait. So, while we are at the pool, my Dad activates my phone or whatever so that he can hear everything!!! Then he hacks every camera at Abby's house and is watching everything!!! I even saw one of his drone pigeons, it waved at me. He ran background checks on every boy at the pool and had an armed guard stationed outside "just in case." And he does stuff like this every day. How do I know you ask? Because he tells me, like, every day. "Always remember, sweetheart, Daddy's watching. Love you!"

So maybe you're like, well, he cares. If that was all he did, maybe I would be okay with it, but wait, there's more. So, I brought a boy home to meet my Dad in person. I'm like, "Hey, Dad, meet Brian." I knew he probably had him on satellite for weeks, but I'm not trying to freak Brian out. So, I'm introducing my Dad to a guy I really like and who likes me, and then, what my Dad says is totally crazy.

He says, "Hi Brian, it is so nice to meet you, but you are actually supposed to marry some other girl, and I am almost certain you, as a potential suitor, will be an unhelpful influence on my daughter. So, I now demand that you see my daughter as only a friend and not as anything more. I am willing to negotiate monetary incentives to keep your relationship with Chloe enjoyable but pure and platonic." At this point, I calmly excuse myself and cry in my room. After all, Dad sees and controls everything I do, so there is no escape. After crying my eyes out upstairs, I tell Brian he should go home. The next day my Dad informs me that I am now betrothed to my soulmate. His name is Chris, a billionaire war hero from New Zealand. He dreams of being a stage actor and wants an actress wife to share that dream with. Look, I'm sure Chris is a great, no, perfect guy. But are you seeing it now? My Dad is a freaking psycho?

And it's not just boys, oh no. Do you know that I have literally never gotten a question wrong on any of my schoolwork? Yeah, ever. How have I pulled that off you ask? It's simple. Before turning in any assignment or test, my Father, who watched everything, tells me what answers I missed. Usually, I just change the answers and get a perfect grade. But when I don't change the answers, he changes them. Yep. He sends one of his lackeys to the school, and the crony changes my answers. I literally can't get less than 100%. Now don't get me wrong, I loved this as a kid. I never had to study, I never worked hard, I just aced everything, and everyone is sure I am a genius. But now, it is infuriating! I don't grow. I can't grow! I can't really learn. Because I am not really the one being graded; he is. I am not the one doing the assignments; he is. Before I even realize there is a mistake, it is fixed. I am not learning to make good choices because I never really make any choices. And if you think Dad is bad, wait till you get a load of Mom.

So, my Mom is a trip. She is constantly talking about what I should be doing and how I should be doing it. And don't get me wrong, everything she says and does works. I mean, I think she might be an angel… or the devil. In any case, this woman is blessed by some powerful force. She never gets lost, always knows what to say; always has the perfect probing and disarming question that shuts down any disagreement, and she never shuts up. Anything that I do that is not "optimal," that's her favorite word, "optimal." Anything I want to do that is not optimal, she refutes. And refutes WITH DETAILS. Anything I believe, learn about, or even casually think, she breaks down and explains to me what is optimal. Now don't get me wrong, she constantly does kind, loving things for me. She buys me whatever I need or even want most of the time. She makes all my food, washes all my clothes, makes sure that everything in the house is clean, and I mean spotless. Like I have literally never done a chore, on my own, in my life. I never have to clean up my own messes, let alone someone else's mess. Anytime I'm done playing with something or using something, my Mom or one of her maids comes and cleans it up. If I ever actually put anything away and do so beneath her specifications, either she or one of the maids immediately fixes it. And this doesn't just happen with chores. She does this for my food intake, my exercise routines, my time studying, my time at church, my time with friends… She is constantly helping me so that I am always at "optimal."

Everything I do, she has optimized. I think I wrote earlier that I'm a stage actress. But would you believe that I'm also a gymnast, a world-class singer and a magician? How can I do all this? I have been optimized. I can sing every note on a piano. No lie, every note! I can even use my voice as a dog whistle. It's actually the finale of my magic routine where I summon dogs to the stage and have them twirl about me while I sing "part of your world" from the little mermaid. It's a big hit.

I literally look like the best parts of six movie stars. I have over one hundred million followers on Instagram. I'm on posters, magazines, music videos, you name it: everything about my body is perfect. And that should all be amazing, except it's all my mother's doing. She set up and managed all of my accomplishments. Everything I do is adjusted to be optimum. Like, for instance, I got my dad's brown eyes, which according to my mom, were less than optimum. So, of course, I got an extremely expensive surgery which changed my eye color. Now, I really wanted green eyes. I told my mother and guess what. She had four independent studies pulled from her purse and placed them in my lap, all of which confirmed that blue eyes were the most popular eye color and, thus, monetarily more valuable, and therefore "optimal."

So, I have blue eyes. My life is perfectly safe. I am never sick. I am always successful because, technically, I have never failed. Everything about me is always attractive; everyone who sees me either wants me or wants to be me. My life is always eventful; I am always wherever everyone wants to be. I have tickets in my name at every concert, seats at every movie premiere, and a table at every award ceremony. I am in every paper and magazine and TV show and always at the perfect time. I am THE it-girl; literally, 17 Magazine has called me the most it-girl in history. I am perfect.

But not really.

Because I haven't actually done any of these things. I haven't actually done a single thing in my entire life. Oh yeah, and if you're wondering why you're not reading any inappropriate language, it's because I literally have a chip in my brain that does not allow me to form a swear word. Yep, that's right. I can't even cuss. And look, I'm not saying that my parent's decisions for me aren't the best. They really might be. I mean, everything works, right? Like, nothing ever goes wrong or turns against us.

We have more money and friends and power and, like, everything, this year than we did last year and the year before that and, like, every year. And that includes me. Every year, I am more everything good and distanced from everything bad. My parents are definitely not trying to hurt me. The reason I am finding myself hating them, the reason I am going out of my mind, is that I am, like, an observer in my own life. I don't call my own shots… ever. I would just yell at my parents if I thought it would do any good. I'd say, "Why did you make me? Why am I here at all if you're just going to live my life? Like, I'm not saying you guys aren't, like, better than everyone else, but what am I here for? Yes, you can do everything better than I can, I guess, but then just get me out of the equation?

You don't need me, and you clearly don't want me to do anything, so why am I even here?"

It's infuriating! Can you imagine living your life but never really doing anything? Like you're just an extension of your parents? There doesn't seem to be any place where they stop, and I begin. Like, I say "like" all the time. Is that because I learned to say that watching reality TV, or did my parents have me watch it so I would use the perfect language for the perfect image they created for me? Like, do you see how controlling all this is? I'm a slave, not even. I'm basically a robot. A perfect, sexy, wealthy robot. The perfect fish in my dad's perfect fish tank. I look like I have the best life, but, in reality, I have no life at all.

Chapter Three

The Visionary

I was slumped in my recliner, eyes barely open as the Steelers played the Baltimore Ravens on Sunday Night Football. I worked nights Thursday and Friday and was more than a little ticked that at my age I was still getting up on roofs for installs. I love solar panels, it's good work and good pay, but even after all these years I still didn't have a reliable crew. My muscles ached. Almost every thought for a week had been about Steelers and Ravens, and now I couldn't even focus on them. My eyelids were weighted and my mind foggy. My cat jumped on me, and I jolted. I grabbed a Coke to keep me awake, and it went to work almost immediately. But the game itself could not sustain the caffeine burst. Halftime hit, and my beloved Pittsburgh Steelers were only leading by three. 3-0, to be exact. It was a punt festival, and my brain was about to punt me into

Monday. I almost got out of my Lazy Boy to grab a wooden chair from the kitchen, but that seemed excessive I just needed another Coke. This was the biggest game of the year, and I was not gonna miss it. As I opened the fridge, I looked at my beat up, calloused hand and thought, "Shoulda stayed in school." I got back in my seat and got comfortable with the cat. Too comfortable. I fought through the halftime show and got to the third quarter, but as the field correspondent explained the adjustments each team needed to make, my eyes became too heavy, and sleep overcame me.

When I awoke, I was looking down at a man sitting with his eyes closed, alone, in the center chair of a movie theater. I began to descend towards the man. As I was lowered, I somehow realized that this man had been sitting in this chair all his life. I found the thought ridiculous, since the man looked perfectly healthy. But the idea imposed itself so fittingly and firmly that I was unable to resist it. As I came close to the man, I drifted slightly to his right and faced him from the side. Suddenly, lights flashed from every direction. My eyes were slapped by an ocean of bright colors. When my eyes adjusted, I found myself inside the most realistic and immersive 3D experience possible: I was sitting above a giant grassy plain covered in African animals. Moving at insane speeds, I passed hundreds of different animals. I stopped abruptly in front of a lion. I began to slowly contort around the lion seeing, in vivid detail, his fur, claws, mane, and teeth. Each individual hair shone in the African sun. He shook his mane and the dust motes flew. His eyes shone with reflected light, but he never saw me. I smelled his breath; I heard a fly whizzing past his mane. I reached out to touch him, but like any 3D image, my hand simply ran through the light. The scenery was all around me. Then I saw dozens of other animals: a zebra, rhino, giraffe, hyena, and an elephant. This wasn't like being in a zoo. These animals were wild and had all the features of freedom, and through this 3D experience, I watched them more closely than any zoo would have allowed. After what felt like hours, I noticed I was still sitting next to the man and his eyes had opened.

He was motionless next to me. The only body part that moved were his eyes, and they moved quickly. His eyes must have had many experiences like this: they were attuned to the scene in front of us, and clearly captured more of what was happening than mine. I tried to talk to the man, but he gave no indication that he could hear me. I got up to move my hand across his face, but he did not appear to notice. I reached out to touch him but then hesitated; it might be dangerous to disrupt someone from a trance or hypnotic state. But curiosity got the best of me, and I moved my hand to touch him. Before I made contact, however, a voice boomed all around me. It said, "Sit." Scared out of my mind, I shot to my seat like a thunderbolt. And then suddenly I heard the voice again, deep, and full as a horn, yet loud and blasting like a trumpet. It spoke with great patience and exactitude. The voice was not singing, but somehow it sounded like music.

Divine Hiddenness

"Behold," stormed the voice, "I am the one, the only who is from the beginning. There was nothing before, and there is nothing beyond me. Watch and see if you can, the work I have done. Stare and be amazed. For you have been given eyes that see. Watch and wait until isolated vision reveals it's blindness."

I felt the voice leave and I was made to see a plant—a small flower. It had a bright yellow bed and firm pink outline. It smelled like the morning. After feasting my eyes and nose I was given sight to see within the plant: its cellular structure and organization. Time sped up. Each cell was perfectly obedient in its role, each movement calculated, all things working toward the plant's good.

I was then taken to watch various animals. Mice and tigers, giraffes and dogs, bears and lizards. I watched, and I watched. Questions gradually filled my mind the longer I looked at each animal. Why do tigers hunt alone while lions hunt in packs? How have giraffes survived as long as they have? How can there be so many types of lizards? But as curiosity grew, so did delight. I experienced the chill of two rhinos at war, the sweetness of elephant fathers teaching their sons, the awkward intelligence of an ape cracking nuts with rocks. I was made to understand each cardiovascular, respiratory, intestinal, nervous, bone, cellular, and atomic structure.

I was made to see waterfalls and mountains, forests and deserts, oceans of water alongside the land, and oceans of lava beneath it. I saw the center of the world, with all of the metals and rocks strewn throughout it. I was shown the

Laws, the invisible powers that govern our world. I could see the magic and not just its effects. I watched the Mighty One, the One who made the invisible power, change, and restructure the Laws to create new marvels. His Word was Law, and all things happened according to this Law. As I watched, I lost all sense of time, and I could not tell if it had been one hour or one millennium. There was always more to watch, revealing new details I had missed at first.

I was taken into the sky and moved at incredible speeds across the cosmos. Light and dark wove around me, and I was terrified. I wanted to shut my eyes, but I couldn't. As I watched, my eyes adjusted, and I began to enjoy soaring through a swirl of light and darkness. I slowed as I approached a new planet that also had a blue sky. I saw storms and lightning. I saw the Mighty One place lightning, thunder, wind, hail, and snow about Himself. I saw hurricanes and tornadoes, tsunamis and earthquakes, fires, and Eruptions. I watched rainbows form, and then the Master moved them across my body. I felt the light about me. The light came to form a feast, such as I had never seen. Meats and cheeses, breads and wines, fruits and seeds, and foods I had never seen before. As the food and drink passed through me, I tasted it. It somehow filled my mouth, and I ate and drank. No matter how much I consumed I was not full, and neither was I hungry. I just enjoyed all that was given to me.

I was taken to a high mountain where the Great One built an altar and temple. With His skill and wisdom, He built a castle one hundred miles tall, reaching beyond the atmosphere, linking heaven and earth. From the pinnacle, He took me to other parts of space. I saw planets and stars, nebulae and meteors, all different types of light in all different kinds of galaxies. I watched Him do great deeds. He wrapped Himself in the lights; He spun nebulae into a spiral. From His breath came a star, and from His hands came water upon waterless planets. I watched and watched and watched and watched. And all the while, the voice said, "I am the glorious One, the Great One, the only Good One. I and I alone am worthy of the highest praise. See my goodness if you can. See my greatness if you can. See my glory if you can. Watch and see, if indeed you have eyes." He said many other things that I cannot remember.

Then His voice fell silent, and the light show ended, and I was again in the theater with the man. I was breathing heavily, and I noticed that tears had been steadily falling down my face. I had never seen so much beauty at one time. I must have been a strange sight: Hands fixed on the arms of the chair, eyes wide, mouth wide, tears flowing, snot flowing, smiling big, drool hanging. Quite a sight indeed. My heart was bursting through my chest. After what felt like hours my mind began to come down and my heart began to fall. And as it did, I became gradually aware that it had been pierced by something. I felt alone. Strangely alone; As if a woman that I loved had forgotten about me or my family had died. And I realized I wanted to hear the voice again. I wanted to hear the music. I wanted to feel it shake my bones. I was pierced by some kind of longing. I felt empty, so empty, I might have tried to consume anything to get full again. But then something healed me. I felt something invisible come over me and soothe me and I was made normal again.

I noticed the man to my left anew. He appeared to be sleeping-but other than being slightly more relaxed and having his eyes closed, he had not moved. I decided to inspect him. There was no excess fat and no wrinkles—a common-looking man in his mid-thirties. I looked around to see if anyone else was in the theater, but we were alone. I suddenly sensed that it was okay to touch the man. Not wanting to disobey the voice, I tried to reject the sense. Suddenly, the voice spoke again, very softly though, just above a whisper: "Touch the man, my son. Touch him and discover who and why he is." I breathed sweet air as I heard the voice again. And at its instruction I touched the man's arm. Suddenly the projections returned, and we were swept away to another planet. Everything was frozen, and everything was beautiful. A giant crystal castle. And yet, somehow, vegetation thrived. I moved to the edge of my seat waiting to learn what kind of molecular structure such plants must have. My eyes widened with anticipation waiting to discover what unique vegetable life could survive on this blue world. But suddenly, I was moved to a seat just behind the motionless man and The voice said, "Watch now my son, watch and know the gifts you have been given."

My seat was higher and right behind the man. The 3D images still surrounded both of us but now at all times the man was in my view. We started inspecting the different plants. I marveled at the different kinds of plant life. A flower seemingly made of ice. Some sort of vinyl plant that climbs up ice walls and melts them. An extremely tall tree that absorbs nearby clouds and vapor. As we descended beneath the ice exterior, we came to a warmer rock interior. Lava and water poured on either side of rock pathways. And it was here that for the first time we saw animals. My heart rose as we neared what looked like a 10-foot-tall white stick creature. But then, suddenly, I heard a new voice break the silence like a siren. A voice as unlike the Great One's voice as can be imagined. Nasally and pinched it squeaked out as if to harm ear drums. "Here we go," it snickered. I looked for where the sound could have come from, and then I heard it again. "It's the same every time when I see these types of things." The voice seemed to be coming from the man. I walked around to the front of his chair so that I could see his face and introduce myself. While I moved, I heard the voice again. "Ok, yes, I see it." The noise was coming from the man, but he was not moving at all. All that was moving were his eyes, which were once again open.

I tried to wave my hand in front of him. I nudged him, but still, nothing stirred apart from the motion of his eyes. I heard the man's voice again, "Here we go again, another new planet. Oh, and this one is covered with ice. It's only the 800th of this kind that I have seen." I stared at him awhile and then looked up to see that we were still under the planet's icy exterior, watching a most magnificent underground

The Visionary

waterfall. Under an icy roof the waterfall fell into a river which wound along miles of imposing stone. I was enraptured, but my awe was interrupted by the most ridiculous nonsense I had ever heard. "Oh well, another waterfall. I bet it... yep, it flows into a river. If I've seen one, I've seen them all. I bet now I'm going to get a full tour of the subterranean areas of this planet, and... as predicted, the tour begins." The voice was unpleasant, the words were revolting.

Did this idiot not realize how amazing this all was? The voice continued, "Oh wow, there are worm creatures in this underground maze... I bet they are the ones building it, and... they are tunneling worms." He groaned, "The planet's center, and it's a molten metallic hybrid, like every third planet." As I listened, I was angered and intrigued. "Every third planet," I thought, "he has seen planets that are not like that at their center? But while my curiosity peaked, my anger burned. The man continued to profane every visible thing with a weak and disinterested tone until I could stand it no longer. "What kind of thing are you," I finally said aloud. I wanted to leave. And then I heard the voice of the Great One, "The thing you see before you is not what it appears to be. He is not human and exists for your benefit so that you may know what it is to have eyes and not see. That you may know what eyes you have been given. Watch him, and you will understand."

When the voice had finished speaking, I readied myself to listen to this "un-man" speak. I watched what he watched and listened to what he said. Somehow knowing that he was not really a human made things easier. As night fell, we watched the most magnificent snowbird. She was enormous, at least twenty feet tall, with wings so large that thick snowfall did not hinder her flight in any way. She was white and blue with dark silver talons only slightly lighter than polished tungsten. The power of her wings hurled entire clouds into vapor. When she rose above the clouds into the soft light of her planet's very distant blue giant, she gleamed. She flew and twisted, full of majesty and color. The blue light shone violet off the gloss of her wings, and in that light, I could see the tiny streaks of silver.

As we watched this unparalleled creature, I could hardly maintain my composure listening to what the un-man said. "I wonder how long we are going to watch this thing," he said, with sarcastic disdain. "Another one with wings. I bet it flies. There it goes. So predictable. I see a mouth. Does it squawk? Yep. God, I hate that noise. The bigger they are, the more annoying the sound. Typical." After a while, the animal went to see its family hidden in a cave. The mother was feeding its young with big green berries. Lava flowed through the cave which kept the giant birds warm. Meanwhile, the bleating continued. "Of course, it has a family. How nice. I bet we were going to watch them eat. Typical."

"Typical" had to be the un-man's favorite word. We saw mountains "typical," wild beasts "typical," exotic fruits, "typical," blazing volcanoes "typical." We moved on to other planets, constellations, and nebulae and for hours every marvel we encountered was, "typical." At last, I could take it no longer, and I called to the Great voice, "Please, let me leave. I can't take this anymore."

I heard nothing for a while and resigned to continue watching and listening. But then we were to the frontier of our universe, watching space expand revealing vast voids. There was nothing to see for some time, then I saw something moving. And suddenly, I knew the Mighty One was making something. I watched as he pulled something through what seemed to be a dark hole in space and colorful gasses appeared. Then abruptly, I heard the jarring voice of the un-man. "Here we go again; he's making something. Bet I can guess what it is. It's either a star or a planet. I'll just have to wait, like always. Well, come on already, get going." The Mighty One began to speed up His work, and slowly, the cloud of gas condensed. We waited and watched, and then unexpectedly, the Mighty One lit the flame, and stars burst forth. Giant burning stars emerged, consuming more and more gas. I was astonished. My companion… "Stars. Yep. Typical."

"Is this thing incapable of joy?" I thought, "Does he have any clue what power is on display? Let's see him make a star or a planet or animals or anything!" I became angry and started thinking out-loud. "What have you ever done? You just sit there and watch and complain. You don't know what you're looking at! I spent twenty-five years building a business that developed solar panels. Me and hundreds of other people work sixty-hour weeks just trying to harness the power of one of these things. And this Mighty One produces them like bonfires. I have wanted to see the Grand Canyon my entire life, but I have never been there because of work. Now, I have seen things that I never even dreamed were real. Why don't you appreciate this?" And as I said the words, it hit me. "Because you've never done anything."

When this thought crept in, a mental dam broke, and a surge of ideas rushed into me like a living river. "I appreciate strength because I have experienced weakness. I appreciate animals because I've lived with them. I look at the stars in wonder because I have lived a lifetime on a tiny planet. I'm fascinated by color because I've tried to paint. I marvel at the flight of the snowbird because I am flightless. I am impressed at the tediousness of ecosystems because I have both succeeded and failed to create far simpler and less volatile systems myself. I see what he cannot, because I live, and he only observes."

I stood speechless. My life, for one moment, made sense. This man's life is pain-free, want-free, fear-free. But also hope-free, love-free, courage-free, wisdom-free, patience-free, kindness-free, faithfulness-free, discipline-free, and joy-free. He was spared many things, and also sheltered from many things. He watched the Maker do great things but was given no great things to do himself. He could not appreciate greatness because he had never tried to be great. He could not enjoy or even appreciate life because, although he was alive, he was not living. A brain he had, and though he lived in a body, his life was not embodied.

The Visionary

His body, free from all work, was also free from all usefulness. I looked down at my hands and feet and had never been more thankful for them. I had never realized how much understanding I owed to my body.

I looked at the un-man again, and as I did, there was a flash, and the vision ended.

Chapter Four

Growing Up

At the house down the street and around the corner from where you currently live, an older man is growing up. Now, make no mistake, the man is a grown-up. But ya know; there really is no such thing as a grown-up, just people growing up. And today, this story is about a hero who learns this lesson again. So please make yourself comfortable and, perhaps, with some tea, listen to the not-so-long story of Mr. Ben MacGuffin.

Now, when Mr. MacGuffin was a boy, he was like any other boy for the most part. He played games, got into trouble, was much too muddy around the house, and ate plenty of sweets. But, in one way, he was somewhat peculiar. Mr. MacGuffin, Benny as he was then called, had the most curious habit. Any time he saw someone perform a task successfully, he believed he could do the job just as well, especially if he had never done the thing himself. His mother first noticed Benny's habit when she baked him a cake for his 5th birthday. After everyone had finished singing to him, Benny's first words were, "Really mum, a one-layer cake? I would have made a skyscraper of a cake!" This was not the first time Benny had said something so precocious, but, from that moment on, no one ever ceased to notice. His first time at Wimbledon, he watched the men's qualifying rounds for no fewer than 10 minutes when he leaned over and said to a fellow nine-year-old.

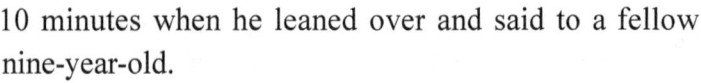

"I don't see what everyone is on about, of course these guys can hit the ball look how big that racquet is." He watched his father shoot skeet, and after hitting two clay pigeons and missing the third, he exclaimed, "I wish they'd hand me the gun; at a hundred pellets a shot how can you miss these things?" At 14, Benny's father spent a small fortune transporting his family to Utah to attend game six of the NBA Finals. This game was none other than Micheal Jordan's finest and final hour as a Chicago Bull.

He watched as the legend strode towards the rim, crossed back, lept in the air, and lofted the ball into nothing but net. With only 5 seconds left the Utah Jazz were stunned and dejected. Utah's fans, however, found themselves cheering for their opponent, overawed by his greatness. Amid the uproar, Mr. MacGuffin reached his hands towards the heavens and in anguish prayed, "Oh Lord, if only it had been me, I would have dunked it."

Such was the life of Mr. Ben MacGuffin. Until, one day, after consuming his mother's blueberry pie, he said, "Nice try, mum, but next time a little softer crust, will you?" At this supreme hour, Mrs. MacGuffin had, had enough. She commanded that her son make his own pie right there. At first, stunned at his mother's command, Benny regained himself and retorted, "Well then, I shall! Where is the recipe?" Being a fair woman, his mother gave him the recipe and showed him where she kept all the ingredients. And behold, at the ripe age of 15, Benny made his first blueberry pie—or at least something trying to be a blueberry pie. In truth, what he made in just under four hours was a sort of blueberry soup with some bread-like substances floating about. The effect of pulling this disaster out of the oven cannot be overstated. It was as if a thunderbolt had struck his brain. This- was nothing short of a revelation.

Sadly, the power of revelation lasts only a brief period for all men. His poor mother, believing to have effected real change, could not believe her ears when, after hearing his older cousin's piano recital, her son exclaimed, "Piano's the easiest instrument. If I started playing the piano, I'd have mastered this piece inside of an hour." His mother, notably frustrated, accosted the young man afterward, exclaiming, "Didn't you learn anything from the blueberry incident?" To her astonishment, her son exclaimed, "What's that got to do with this?" She tried to explain, but Benny simply retorted, "Blueberry pies are more complicated than I thought, and I credit your abilities now mother, but, what has pie got to do with piano?" After an hour, his mother realized there was nothing for it.

Now you might feel that this story can only end badly for the psychologically impaired MacGuffin, but that is where you would be wrong. Mr. MacGuffin just had a long road to discovery. As fate would have it, Mr. MacGuffin found himself around people with the fighting spirit of his mother for the rest of his life. Different people challenged him to make good on his ignorant promises—to do what others had worked so hard to accomplish. And time and again, Mr. MacGuffin found the craft more difficult than he initially surmised. And gradually, something remarkable happened; he became a hard worker.

The first task he worked hard at and eventually mastered was plumbing. At 18, he told his parents' plumber that his job was mundane and ordinary and that he took far too long in doing it. The plumber then obliged, "Well guv, if it's so ordinary then, why don't you do it yerself." Mr. MacGuffin agreed, and the plumber was dismissed. Mr. MacGuffin found the job almost infinitely more challenging than he had imagined, but he worked tirelessly to master it over the next four years.

The next thing he learned was how to consume a massive number of hot dogs in one sitting. He was on holiday in America when he came upon the National Hotdog Eating Competition and witnessed none other than history's most prolific eater of hotdogs, Mr. Joey Chestnut. It was after seeing Joey Chestnut tie his own record, eating 68 official Nathan's Hotdogs, that Mr. MacGuffin exclaimed, "Bosh, how big's a hot dog after all?" He proceeded to throw up after eating a mere six. However, five years later, after training his body to consume hot dogs, Mr. Benjamin MacGuffin qualified to compete in the annual Coney Island Games, challenging none other than the immortal Joey Chestnut. Mr. MacGuffin was handily defeated by Mr. Chestnut, who, broke his own record, devouring 72 official Nathan's Hotdogs. Nonetheless, Mr. MacGuffin fared much better than before, himself consuming 41 hotdogs—obviously a tremendous improvement. Mr. MacGuffin's heart burned from the acidity of the hot dogs, but it burned even more from his love for Mr. Chestnut. The two embraced after the closing ceremony with tears of admiration, then promptly puked upon one another.

After this day, Mr. MacGuffin began to suspect the unimaginable complexity of almost everything in the universe. His natural disposition had not wholly shifted, but the shift had begun. The more he knew, the more he knew he didn't know. The more he learned the more he learned there was more to learn. For the rest of his life, including today, Mr. MacGuffin invested his efforts fully in various passions, hobbies, and studies, the end result of which was always the same—an earned appreciation for the endeavor.

These appreciations had bordered upon the poetical, even the religious, in Mr. MacGuffin's mind. But on this day, today, the appreciation he gained was unmistakably divine. Today, Mr. MacGuffin's grandfather died. Given the disposition of Mr. MacGuffin, one should not be surprised that the following thought crossed his mind, "Well, dying doesn't seem so hard that it deserves this big party?" By party Mr. MacGuffin was referring to his grandfather's funeral and reception. But as the thought entered his mind many of his adventures that are here told, also entered in. He thought of that day when his mother first challenged him to make a pie. He remembered the shock of that soupy dish coming out of the oven, and as he remembered he thought, "I never did figure out how to make a pie." Then he thought of his mothers pies. Masterful dishes they were, the opposite of his few baking episodes. He thought more about his mom and of all the things that she had done for him. He looked over and saw his mother crying as she spoke to a friend about her dead father and Ben considered what a wonderful woman she was. He thought of how honestly she loved her father and her children and her husband. And then he thought of all the sacrifices she made for her family, most of all for a stubborn man like him. At that moment a weighty truth settled inside of Ben, "Dying is easy, that's not why we're here, even living is easy if we're selfish, but loving, loving is hard." Hard and good, like everything he had ever learned to appreciate. He looked around at all the crying faces and he knew that death had not called for a party, love did. Tears rolled down Ben's cheeks as he looked at his mother. He imagined the day when he would be in a place like this for her. "I'm going to throw her the biggest party in the world."

Chapter Five

Grandfather

Kenneth Kathy slowly walked to his car. It was not a hot day, and he had been in an air-conditioned room for the last two hours; yet, pearls of sweat formed across his brow. Kenneth could not wait to get in his car and drive away, far away, far enough that no one who knew him would find him.

His son and family exited the restaurant, and his eldest grandson waved at him and yelled, "Goodbye, Grandpa." It took all his energy to look at the boy he loved, smile and wave back. The boy's round face stung his heart. As he turned again to move towards his car, he found himself with less energy and moved even slower. He wanted to become invisible so that he could curse as loud as he could or lie down and weep or hit something. He kept clenching and unclenching his fists.

His mind had no home, it ping-ponged between rage and despair so quickly that all he consistently felt was exhaustion. He started his car and turned the A/C to full blast as if it would cool down his burning heart. After five minutes, his mind homeless, his head down and eyes closed, he said five words to God. He put the car in drive and left the parking lot. He knew where he was going.

He hated that he had to get out of his car to find an attendant to open up the gate. But he moved quicker, having some physical and emotional distance from the restaurant. The attendant opened the gate, and Ken got back in his car and drove up the beautifully manicured pathway.

It took only two minutes of driving uphill to find the spot. He knew where he was going. "Mary Kathy 1949-2018," the flowers on her grave were still yellow as they were the previous day when he had left them. Ken, feeling much better now that he was near his best friend, became himself again. He sat on the ground in front of the grave, took a few moments, and began to speak to his wife.

"Hi honey. Today's been another hard day. It was the kids again. Well, not all the kids, the usual kid. I know what you'd say, so it's not like I don't, but it was always easier for you so…" He paused, realized he was rambling, and remembered that Mary hated when he rambled, so he collected his thoughts and tried again. "I'll just get to the point. It's Manny, I just know he's screwing up, and I don't know what to do. Lord, you know I have prayed. God can tell you honey, I have prayed, cuz I know you would say that.

You would tell me to pray for him... well, I have Mary. But Manny just isn't interested in what anyone has to say. Not me, not Pastor John, not even God, I don't think." Ken's back was uncomfortable, so he sat up against a tree, facing Mary's grave. He had done this before, and as usual, this helped him sit more comfortably.

"He's messing up our grandkids hun. He has two beautiful boys; God, I wish you could see 'em. The oldest is 10 now, and he's twice as bold as when you saw him last. But they barely know their Dad. I mean, he doesn't *do* anything with them. He is at work constantly. When he is not working, he is out with his friends, and on the rare occasion when he is home, he watches TV or plays those stupid video games." His blood began to boil as he spoke, and he knew that if Mary had seen this happening, she would have interrupted with a "Kenneth, you're becoming emotional." So, he calmed himself down and began again. "They're not going to church. I mean, once in a while, they go, but it's not a priority. I had to ask them to come with me for Father's Day. His kids know more about Paw Patrol and the Avengers than the Old Testament. You talk to Manny's kids, and then you talk to Josiah's kids; you'd think you were talking to the children of an atheist and an orthodox Jew. Manny's kids are just not learning anything that matters. He doesn't teach them anything. They know about sports teams and video games. But they don't know the Bible or math or even the difference between a flat head and a Phillips." He paused again, once more realizing his need to calm down.

"Sometimes, I just want to come in there and take those kids away. Raise them myself. It's not a crazy idea. Guys my age have done it before." As he said this he looked up at the soft clear blue of the afternoon. The sky seemed farther away for some reason. He stared at it as if somehow by staring he could bring it lower. After some time, he realized he was picturing his friend Terry who was raising his grandkids. But Terry's son had died in a car accident and his daughter-in-law was never the same. "That is nothing like this situation."

He smirked and let out a small laugh, thinking of his wife's somewhat harsh demeanor. "I can hear you saying, 'You have to let them live their lives.' Yeah, I know it's true. I think of the little ice cream business my Dad helped me start and gave me when I turned 16. He said, 'Ok son, it's your business now; whether this business survives or not is up to you.' I remember being so mad at my Dad when it failed, and he wouldn't help me buy more ice cream to sell. A year later, I realized something though. If he had stepped in and took over when I was screwing things up, it would be like he had never given it to me in the first place. It would be 'my' business in name only; the one who actually ran it was still my Dad. He was trying to teach me that, unless I take responsibility for something, it's never really mine. It is only the things that we protect, provide for, work at, think about, plan for, feed and help grow; these are the things that are really ours. It is only by laying our life down for something that we ever really get anything. And it is only *those things* that we ever learn to truly love. That's what my father taught me. And I may never have learned it if I had not been allowed to fail."

Kenneth paused to imagine his wife's face. She was looking at a dish half listening to her husband, who, as usual, was using her as a sounding board to get his thoughts in order. His heart warmed at how patient his wife had been with him throughout their life together. How often she busied herself while Ken talked until he collected his thoughts.

"Thank you, honey. This is usually the part where you give me some more advice." He laughed, then a sober thought crossed his mind. "Losing an ice cream business is one thing. But losing your kids." He paused to hold back tears. "Is it really true that learning responsibility is *this* important?" Tears overcame him, the faces of his grandchildren crowded out all reason. He sat and wept before the Lord. Unknown to him an Angel stood just behind, listening. And since Kenneth had no more words to pray, the angel prayed for him.

"Oh God, you really give us things. I will never accuse you of not meaning what you say. You have given us our lives and so our lives are our own. You have placed inside humanity the potential to be parents and the children they make are their own. You are the Grandfather of them all. You have allowed your children to have children themselves. You will not father all children directly and steal the privilege of fatherhood from them. You will not be a father whose children remain children always. But you allow them to try their hand at fathering like you. To take responsibility for children in a way similar to you. But to accomplish this you must remove yourself and not fix every failure. You are the mightiest thing in existence, so mighty you can restrain even yourself. For humanity either takes responsibility, or they do not. You cannot do that for them. But Lord, their failures are great, and it is so hard to learn responsibility. Please be merciful to the offspring of those who create children but neglect to raise them."

Chapter Six
Rules of War and Boundaries of Love

To my loving father, Gabriel, upon Fulcundra the sapphire, to the namesake and father of all that is fair upon that world, and to Nethunas The Deep freedom in Arřu.

Thankfulness and joy surround me as my thoughts turn to you. For years beyond number, we shared the honey of wisdom and set ourselves to cultivate the oceans of Neptune. We planted the forests in the sea and taught the fish to feed them and the birds to love them. We discovered the treasures hidden by Aaleldil; what tireless years we spent loving and mothering every inch of that world My heart often escapes to that pleasant century when you mentored me as we rooted the island to the heart of Fulcundra. Oh Fulcundra, where each year is strengthened

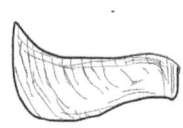

by the previous. A deep world patient and wise. A people old and strong. I will dream of her until Arřu leads me home.

But here at my post, I watch and wait. So few victories, so few battles. I watch, I wait. I have been here for over two hundred earth years; what would feel like a sunrise upon Fulcundra has felt like the most prolonged age of my life.

So many things have been born, and so many things have died. Voices raised, voices silenced, and all came to nothing. Nothing here is bred with patience and love. Everything is hasty. I have never seen such work in all my life. They toil so hard, for there is no time for them to struggle sweetly. Death marks all that they do; it is their enslaver. Decisions must be made, and made quickly, for they will live but 80 of their earth years, and many of those will be eaten by childhood, disease, misfortune, sin and finally in the saddest of all their curses 'old age.' Nothing marks them with futility more than this last paradox. Had never seen anything like it before I came. Age is the pathway to our glory; it is the great gift of Arřu. But here in the fallen world, the path is cut short. Where age always honors us with wisdom and strength it grants them this pleasure only a short while. Before long, it besets them in a ring of every calamity imaginable. And what's worse, their 80 years may be cut short in a moment. To see Aaleldil's plans brought to this, I want to leave daily, but I watch this abomination and wait.

When I was called up to take my post in the war, I thought war would be my primary duty. But so rarely have I waged it. So infrequently has my training been tested, though I prepared for millennia. I make no complaint against this; the trial was sweet, and I am better for it. But my wisdom now fails me.

So I am writing to you, my father. A question burns in my mind, and it is a question I cannot answer. I think about it all day long, and it gnaws against my will to obey the Lord. The ages of men are so swift. Most humans spend their days learning fashions that are discarded merely a year after they are understood. In only two hundred years, I have seen the rise and fall of hundreds of conventions that have claimed the lives and devotions of billions. What they call an age is so short we would not call it anything, for we would not devote a marker of time to something so inexact and fleeting. But I have seen something arise in this present "age" of men that has made the question in my mind so stark and poignant that I must have my father's wisdom to guide me. The Lord speaks so little here. His word is upon my heart, but His wisdom is farther than my eyes yet see. But your eyes are older and stronger than mine. Tell me what you see and answer my tormenting riddle: "I have power to do so much, and yet I am commanded to do so little."

In this present age of men, it seems, the culmination of the Enemy's plans has come. The Enemy works even faster than men. His ways are even more indiscernible. Even his underlings cannot see his plans, for they are always catching up to his designs. But the Enemy has slowed and encircled a land and a people. He is spending his strength again upon a champion of his choosing. And it seems that the strongest of mankind is on the brink of raising amongst them a tyrant in the center of the Enemy's will. And yet my orders have not changed. With some exceptions, I watch and wait.

Father, I know that I speak in ignorance. I babble like a child. But please lend me your ear if only to shoulder the burden of your beloved son. The Enemy is so weak. Our race is robust and numerous. I had read since my youth of our great victories over him when the Adversary was one hundred times his current strength. For all his cries of freedom, he has ensured his bondage, and Michael's chain waits for him. Even I, small as I am among the Eldillea, could bring to justice most of the wraiths I have met here. Yet, I merely watch as they torment men and women. They laugh at me, seeing the pain and love I feel for the humans they haunt. So often, I could end it. But I stick to my orders, and my passion for our Lord keeps me from haste. But my mind falters. I know of the Seventh Law. I know that our fair Master will not send down the Powers of deep heaven until the end of all things. But why do we not wage war as the Enemy does? Even as I speak, I know there must be wisdom in it, for the Enemy cannot but deceive himself. But I am not wise enough to see the deception. So I ask you, father, why do we, or better, why does Aaleldil not end the torment? Why does He not fight the Enemy openly Himself? Why does he not simply undo what the humans have done? The stakes are so high and their salvation so precious to Him; why does He not fight, or at least allow us to fight openly that they might be recovered?

I speak as a fool, but not to a fool. I know that Aaleldil's ways are higher than ours. I understand and will not doubt that there are answers for my soul and will nourish myself upon His goodness as I trust and obey. I *will* wait. I *will* watch. I will trust that the Lord of all the earth will do right. I will see the goodness of Arřu and wait for His freedom. For His voice is from beyond the world. His light from behind the sun. His designs wind and unwind. The purifying flame is all around us and within us. I will remember that faith is not reserved for mortals only for it is the very language of Love.

In Love,
Your Son

2

My dear son, whom I love and with whom I am pleased,

Greetings from the hosts of light and He that is. I pray for you daily and was encouraged to receive word from you as an answer to my prayers. I have discussed your letter with Fulcundra upon your request, and she has confirmed and deepened what Aaleldil has put in my heart. Your word has come to me as my own words once came to Michael before the upending of the world. Your mind is dark, and so was mine. Your sight is short, and so was mine. But your faith is strong, and so was mine. For what you have said was placed in your heart in the fullness of time, and it did not come to your mind from Cecmundi but from beyond the field of Arbol. From that very light behind the sun. Though ignorant, you spoke truly. Obedience unsheathes the creator's sword and a prophet will speak more truth than he knows. This message, long-awaited, has arrived I trust, at the end of a great battle within. This message, slow enough to strengthen and fast enough to succeed, will now confirm the purpose for your perseverance. If your journey was anything like mine, you already know much of what is written here. It would be unnecessary, except to confirm that your prayers were heard.

Your inquiry about the humans upon Cecmundi is difficult to explain since we see as the Father sees, and they see with eyes as they have. They are not what we are. They are amphibious creatures having both a spirit and a body. And what is more, they are born into evil and internally at war all their lives. This first difference is difficult to learn but, when understood, brings light into the soul. The second difference is one Arřu never intended and led to harsh toil. They are not only not what we are; they are not what *they* are. There is now a contradiction within their own nature. They have forsaken the way of men and have become less than men. Even the redeemed are but children. They consider someone an elder as they reach a hundred years. Their life is short, and as their wisdom grows, their bodies fade. It is a wretched life and a sadness so deep I found myself wanting to join them in sleep if only to avoid looking at their faded and fading glory. But I watched them without ceasing as our Father has and bore their burden in the ways that I could, as I trust you have done.

Since you were a boy, you have heard that Aaleldil will not overpower His lovers. He is free, and He would have nothing less for His creatures than freedom. He gives and does not un-gift. He writes His rules in stone and will not break them even if they break Him. This we know; this we have seen. Thus, the freedom of the will when given from Aaleldil is given without recourse; He will not enslave it though they break His heart and damn themselves. For if He did, if by His might He stretched out and broke their will upon his arm, saving His creatures from death; what would He have saved? But an empty vessel, a body only. The person, the actor, the planner, the decision-maker, the intender, the enjoyer, will have been destroyed. We are not observers but agents, and if our agency is destroyed, we are nothing.

Thus, Aaleldil will convince but not control. He will woo but not rape. He will not destroy our will, even if by it we destroy ourselves. But there is a consequence beyond this. His plans cannot be thwarted, and though He halts the designs of others, He will not unmake them. For if He did, it would be an un-gift. For if, when His creatures sinned or made decisions such as His wisdom would not have made, if He rewound time so as to unmake the creatures choice and correct it, this would destroy the freedom of all His creatures. For we all would become like the puppets of the humans, pretend people. A mere extension of His personality, doing nothing and saying nothing except that which Aaleldil forced into our bodies and mouths.

I speak of things you know. Remembering is no burden, and I hope that setting our minds on Arřu's work will encourage you, especially amidst the meaningless clamor of the humans. So few are their holy ones. So little is their lore. So simple are their Scriptures. I remember exhausting their storehouses of wisdom in a day, reading their Scriptures in an afternoon—so little to learn and yet, for them, so little time to learn it. But one of their prophets wrote, "I have seen a limit to all perfection, but Your commandment is without limit. Oh, how I love Your law! I meditate on it all day long." How wise this man was to trust the little light he knew. So, let us harken unto joy and courage by remembering the Lord God's work.

All creatures were created to exist as Aaleldil does, to live in constant giving and receiving of self-communicative and sacrificial love. This is deep wisdom even among the Eldillea. The Accuser's inability to understand it has catalyzed every war, even the one over which you now stand watch. But for all his accusing, he has not been able to produce a community rivaling that which existed from the beginning. A unity strong enough to bear tortures, strong sufficiently to endure distance and fear. Yet not suffocating. A unity, not a homogeneity. Not a binding that blurs distinctions. A unity that simply holds them together. A unity and a diversity. A unity not of restriction but of freedom.

Freedom and diversity not of rebellion or dissonance but of love. For love keeps both unity and diversity alive. For the lover loves the beloved because she is not he. What he loves of her are those beauties appropriate to her and not to him. Thus, love creates the unity and preserves the diversity. We were made for love, as were the creatures that you serve. Love is costly, requires trust to be chosen, and the Accuser did not embrace it.

Our lost brother grew impatient and, while always needing to be different *from* others, could not tolerate the differences *of* others. He has become very loud and very monotonous. He is doing nothing at the highest volume he can. In his dominion, the weak serve the strong. The fragile lift the firm ever higher, and break under the weight. Only that which is most beautiful is seen. Only they that sing best sing at all. All others watch and applaud and are silenced. But this is not so with our Father. Aaleldil knows that unless we work and build and achieve, no affluent and educated appreciation can grow for good work, good buildings, or excellent achievement. Unless we *try* the master's work, we cannot really *appreciate* the masters' work. And so, glory is enhanced, not diminished by the strong and learned watching, waiting, helping the weak and ignorant grow. But it is not simply for Aaleldil's sake that the simple become wise. For Aaleldil needs not our praise. And though He delights in it as a matter of justice and truth, it is not for this that He made us. It is for love that we were created.

He does not simply create; He is Creator. He does not merely love; He is Love. To be Himself is to overflow into artistry. Now, what does it mean that Aaleldil made creatures like Himself but that He made smaller creators and miniature lovers? Is this not what it means to be like Him? But can any animal make anything with the skill and wisdom equal to Aaleldil? And so, though the One could make all things better than we, He has not done so. For Him, it is a delight to give and to trust. He does not simply desire that we hope in Him; He hopes in us. He does not want merely to be trusted; He desires to trust. He is not simply faithful; He wants faithfulness. He is patient; but He also expects patience, for this is Love. I cannot love alone; I need thou. And so, though Aaleldil can do all better than we, He has created us with purposes and will leave them undone that we might do them. In so doing, He creates a space for us to be like Himself.

Remember, my son; we cannot win heaven's war hell's way. The Enemy desires to consume the earth and become stronger by absorption. His aim is to enhance his own glory by taking theirs for himself. But that is never our Father's aim. His glory is enhanced by their glory. The Enemy is fattening pigs for slaughter. Our King is fathering kings for kingdoms. If any victory for heaven is achieved, it will be by calling the humans to become fully human, not by taking upon ourselves the responsibility that Aaleldil entrusted to them. For that would be to steal their glory; that would be the un-gift.

Be patient my son, be patient. And remember the gift that the Lord God gave the sons of Adam. There are signs for them to see if they will but look closely. But let us not forget these signs ourselves. Consider again the ant and place one in your hand. He crawls all about you moving as quickly as he deems safe. He will traverse your body from left to right if you let him; and yet never discover that you are there. To him, you are only a new terrain. Such is the hierarchy of being. Nothing you can do will help the ant know you, but you can know him. You can study him more intimately than he can study himself. He cannot help you, but you can help him; but not in ways that he will understand. He will not even know that he has received help. A bird can know more, still more a dog, and still more a man. All are different and all have their place. But equally, all have their limitations which Aaleldil has placed within them that they might be what they are; no more and no less. But remember this also, Aaleldil became a man. Such is His revelation. He will appropriate down, but they cannot appropriate up. He will become one of them so as to lead them; but He will not destroy their nature simply to satisfy their curiosity. That would be to un-gift. That would be to destroy their greatest joys, their journey and very purpose. Remember this as you serve the sons of Adam and the daughters of Eve.

But also, remember this for yourself. Did not the Lord cry out Himself, "Why hast thou forsaken me?" It is often when the purposes of Arřu are nearest that He feels farthest away. And the doctor is no different than his patients. You too are lower than He and perhaps, like the ant, you run across your Masters arms, not knowing that you are doing so.

I have spoken upon things which you have long known, and I have more to say, but even as I write, Fulcundra has spoken wisely. And so, about your other questions, I will speak to Michael. Though we have learned much of what you ask, Michael's eyes see farther than ours, and the fate of the Competitor has been given to him. He will know better what to say and at what time.

In Love,
Gabriel and Fulcundra

3

My blessed son, whom I love, who has brought me great joy,

Days of mourning and rejoicing came from your last letter. All upon Fulcundra rejoiced and gave thanks for your work among the peoples of the earth, and through you, many have learned a new love. The love of lost things. The love for redemption. The love of the unlovable. It is a music that strains and is hardest for those who have endured it. Hardest for us who have loved so long and so sadly. As I read your letter memories of my sojourn upon Cecmundi came to me. I was reminded of my time abiding with Israel as they returned from exile. And the words I now write are my remembrances of Michael's words to me. And he spoke to me as I now will write to you. You have waited patiently for Michael's reply but Michael said only one thing to Fulcundra and myself; "Tell him what you know." And so, trusting in the Lord's servant, we will obey.

The questions left unaddressed from your previous letter pertained to the silence of Cecmundi. What they call their "Fall." This shameful reality is, in one sense, difficult to imagine and, in another sense, relatively easy to understand. It is hard to imagine because we have never been so lost or bent. We have never been so isolated. We have never chosen lies. All their tools are broken, and all their roads overgrown with weeds and thorns. Danger not only surrounds them, but it also lives in them. There is none among them whom they can always trust, not even themselves. This is a desolation we have never known. And even those who receive Him, hear Him only through great toil. For us, when the words of Aaleldil come, they are obvious. For us, to speak to Him, what the humans call prayer, is like speaking to anyone else, enjoyable and natural. But they have forgotten His language. The spiritual part of their existence is a complete mystery to them and they do not live long enough nor have souls pure enough to learn anything but basics. They neither have the time nor the inclination to learn from Aaleldil as we do. It is because of this that they experience, not only the normal distance Aaleldil allows for the growing of His creatures; but an unnatural distance.

This is the very nature of the human's "Fall." Their ancestors decided Arřu was untrustworthy. It really is as simple as that. When someone is deemed untrustworthy what can be said? Anything said can be distrusted. What can be done? Anything done can be distorted. If faith in final reality is doubted in preference for something self-referential—there is no recourse except to pull back. To allow, through experience—that longest and most arduous pathway to truth—the effects of one's beliefs. To allow the doubt to run its course and then allow the doubter, the distrustful, the faithless to change their minds.

As one of the kings of Israel wrote, "Speak not in the ears of a fool, for he will despise the wisdom of your words." Adding words of wisdom is useless when wisdom itself is on trial. And so He withdraws.

As mankind realizes their need for Him, as their desire for Him awakes; He reveals His Spirit to theirs. The noise of His approach, deafening to us, is barely heard by these beings whose animal nature has consumed them. The physical has so overwhelmed their spirits that some doubt whether they have a spirit at all. Each generation slips further from the echo of those original humans who knew how to discern His voice. The simple methods He taught them in His earthly life are rarely attended to. Even now we hear Aalendil speak to them. The present generation is surrounded by His voice and almost completely deaf to it, so little gets through. Broken and breaking vessels they are, and so little can be done until after the end. This we trust is true about them, but we cannot know their experience as we know our own.

But in regard to how their confusion operates, it is perfectly simple. They are deceived. They believe untrue things. There is not much to learn because there is not much to know. A lie is just a word that signifies a belief that corresponds to nothing. You can hold the truth in your hand. For if I say, 'this is a sword,' and you take it in your hand, the truth is in your hand. But if I say, "this is a sword," and I give you a spear, then I have lied. But what you hold in your hand is still not the lie but the truth. You hold a spear. The lie is the thing that is not. It is an untruth, which is nothing. Thus, sin is not complicated because sin is simply the pursuit of nothing under the guise of pursuing something. Like trying to hold water with a sieve or catch gravity in a bottle. This is the temptation in all who are of the Earth. Most do not resist, but, even for those that do, they cannot escape the thick jungle of consequences the Accuser and his allies have unleashed.

This is the confusion that mankind has brought on itself. This is their futile and costly arrogance. They have attempted to define goodness and have only learned immorality. The more they personalize holiness, the more they identify with sin. The more they fight for their version of good, the more entrenched they are in evil. For they did not make the world, nor do they control it. They do not know the present in detail, much less the future. With what wisdom can they "define" anything? Arřu alone truly creates, Arřu alone truly sustains. All He makes is His, and all He offers us teaches us. For who has known the mind of the Lord or who has been His counselor? Or who has given a gift to Him that he might be repaid? From Arřu and to Arřu and through Arřu are all things. To Him be glory forever; this is the truth. But mankind has denied the fact, and Aaleldil has allowed them to learn from their mistake.

But Arřu is merciful. For in His love and patience, He provides a foreshadowing. They, like the Accuser, have desired to sit on Aaleldil's throne and be Gods unto themselves. They have desired God's removal and so He has removed Himself; but not entirely. He has not given them exactly what they have chosen but only a taste. He is not entirely gone, simply further from them than He ought to be. He has honored their wishes by giving them a premonition of what they can achieve on their own strength. This is the meaning of death. For they cannot, of their own resources, produce life. Nor can we. All our resources are gifts from the One who is life and gives it freely. All the Accuser or mankind can make is death. And death, in its essence, is nothing.

The culmination of their glorious rebellion *is nothing*.

I need not remind you of what a deep sadness this is to watch, for you observe them without ceasing. Stay faithful my son, and love them, not simply as our Father has loved you, but more; love them as He has loved them. Watch and give aid as the Lord leads. The most painful experience I watched over and over again on Cecmundi was when one of their kind truly desired that Aaleldil meet with them as

He once did before the darkening of their world. The righteous want to see Him. There is so much they do not know. They do not see that for Aaleldil to honor their choices; He must allow their decisions to affect other people; even a people yet unborn. This is mainly invisible to them with concern to future generations. And so, they do not see that Aaleldil cannot honor the decisions of past generations without letting those decisions affect future generations. They do not see that for them and those around them to have meaningful purposes, there must be things that Aaleldil must not do alone. They do not understand that they must receive important tasks or remain infants forever. They have forgotten Aaleldil's language, so their prayers are short, toilsome, and confused. They would avail nothing if Aaleldil's love did not stoop very low. They do not see the Enemy's jurisdiction, which *they* gave him, that prevents many of Aaleldil's desires, for He will not uproot injustice with injustice. They do not understand the rule of faith: the more He reveals Himself, the more complex the trials must be. Since He will never eliminate the need for trust in any of His creatures. They desire importance, not knowing what it means. They are so young and poorly trained that they rarely perceive the difference between the Enemy's efforts and our own. They cannot even distinguish the difference between being distracted by the Enemy and when, for their benefit, Aaleldil removes Himself from their emotional experience. They believe every period of dryness is a mark of the Enemy. When, perhaps a third of them are Aaleldil removing His hand that they may learn to walk.

They do not understand how bent they are. How their evil gives all divine aid two sides. They do not see that if Aaleldil were to speak to them face to face, they would become arrogant, selfish, and lazy. Pride runs so deep that when He reveals His greatness to them, they associate it with themselves. Thinking they are great for being counted worthy of such treatment. They are so selfish that time with Him does the opposite of what it does for us. Where we feel invigorated to love each other for the love of Him. They disdain one another for 'love' of Him. Their selfishness is so profound that the more He meets their needs, the more their 'love' is reserved only for those who meet their requirements. When all along, His plan for them is to love their neighbors and become like Him, needing them less and less while loving them more and more.

Aaleldil desires them to function as a whole in the same way that He structured their individual bodies; each member performing its task in obedience to the head. But the more He does, the less they seek the aid of one another. It is a tangled game which He and we play with men. We remove ourselves so that they need one another in hopes that the joy of unity might inspire them to a lasting unity even when necessity no longer dictates it. But they die so quickly, and the young know the old so poorly. Should Arřu make Himself freely available, the human community would not endure. They would never be a body, never learn the joy and love of submission, and never be like God. Sloth is so deep that the more He gives, the more they expect. Indeed, if Aaleldil became their slave, they would cease using even their bodies for anything but pleasure. And by doing this eventually cut themselves off from every pleasure. They would work against half, if not all, of their purpose. They would hate and deny themselves until they hated and denied Him as the Accuser did. It is for ignorance of these and more profound truths that all on Cecmundi struggle to hear Aaleldil, even those who desire to, even their holy ones.

Aid their holy ones, my son. Help them hear. For they hear so little, and even the loudest of heaven's cries are to them an echo of some beautiful language they have mostly forgotten. Comfort them and give them endless opportunities for humility, for they are not a race that can afford to be proud. So little awareness of themselves and of others and of reality. So little knowledge of things present, past or future, large or small, far or near, within or without. So little wisdom for their life is so short. Aid them, my son, be perfect as your heavenly Father is perfect. Love, for your heavenly Father is love. And see them as He sees them. They desire to journey alone, but He watches them, out of the corner of His eye. He waits for them and grieves for them. I remember watching His tears as He returned from burying His friend in Moab. See them as He sees them. It is hard not to see sadness and failure, but learn to love these unfaithful friends, and you will know the heart of Him that you love and loves you.

In Him,
Gabriel and Fulcundra

4

Dearest Gabriel and to your sister Fulcundra,

I write briefly here because I wanted you to return correspondence to Hector quickly and because there is little to say. But know that my brevity ought not to communicate flippancy; my heart has rejoiced in Aaleldil every moment that I have thought about you both. I will come to you soon as I have asked for leave of my duties to make the journey, and I believe that you both will delight in my coming. Gabriel, my younger brother, I know you will encourage Hector as you would a son, so I will say little of that and speak directly to your inquiry. Tell Hector what I received and passed on to you. The humans under his care are to make every effort to convert their fellows. They ought to, as the Master said, "make disciples of all nations." Like our own efforts, we will not know their efficacy until the end of all things. Neither will we know how important our or their decisions were in terms of results.

We do not know the importance of the missions God gives us, and even less so, the importance of the tasks God gives humanity. It may be that a soul will never be damned due to the failings of humans. As I daily hope and pray, it may be that Arřu will mend all wounds and that all obedience towards the heathen's salvation is more about learning obedience and reducing temporary evil than actually saving the unrepentant. To clarify, my hope is not that Arřu will give salvation to everyone who never wanted it. But instead, that salvation, by His wise hand, will find those who did not know what they always wanted. That Arřu, through His skill and mercy, will save all creatures whose ignorance was their undoing and not rebellion. Thus, in the human situation, Arřu would preserve some people who, through man's negligence and other evils, never bowed to Christ but would have.

Thus, God does what they could have done but failed to do. The external effect, then, of their preaching and our war would be to speed the healing of the repentant. It would be to do quickly and less painfully what Arřu would do at the end of all things. This would create a safety net underneath the tightwire show that is our cosmos. We help those who desire to come to Aaleldil and walk in love, joy, and patience *now*. This reduces current miseries as well as secures their future glory. For this I hope and pray. But irrespective of whether or not this is how the Lord works. What we do know is that the missions He gives us, and even more those He gives humans, are massively important *to us*. It is how we learn obedience. It is how we walk along the narrow road and find the small gate that leads to life. It is how we grow up to be like Aaleldil.

The conversion of the heathen is as much about our hope as it is about theirs. Their conversion teaches us to love them and Him in the most uncomfortable of situations. It proves that we love them, God, and God in them. By desiring their good more than our comfort, we demonstrate holiness with actions that speak far louder than any words. And even if Aaleldil will mend all the failures of His soldiers, their failures will cause their brothers and sisters great pain. Regardless of the situation the glory is ours to offer God if we succeed and it is lost forever if we fail. Have Hector encourage the righteous of Cecmundi with this.

In Love,
The Eldest Brother.

Chapter Seven
Paul and Luke

Today ought to have been a good day for Paul and Luke. They had clear skies, a nice light wind in the direction they needed the ship to go. They ate before they left and enjoyed something other than grain for the first time in over a week. This should have been a relaxing, enjoyable day. But it wasn't. All Luke could think about were Paul's words to their Centurion the previous day, "Our voyage is going to be disastrous and bring great loss to ship and cargo, and to our own lives." Luke had never heard Paul utter anything incorrectly about the future. But the moment the ship's captain heard Paul say this to the Centurion, he took offense. Both the captain and the owner of the ship were not going to let a prisoner steer its course. They scoffed and laughed at Paul, quickly convincing the crew that Paul was out of his depth. The next day they set sail. The sky was blue, the wind was perfect and the crew felt certain that Paul was an arrogant prig. Luke felt embarrassed for his friend, no one could deny that at least for the first day of sailing Paul was wrong. Paul, however, felt no shame.

He had left Luke at the stern and asked the Centurion to take off his chains to make swimming easier should the boat be destroyed. The Centurion laughed, but after Paul insisted, he released his bonds.

While Paul was away, Luke thought anxiously at the back of the ship. Paul's ominous prophecy echoing in his head. Luke was scared- he just knew Paul was going to be right again. But He also didn't want to be made fun of like Paul; and so tried not to show his fear. Most couldn't tell he was afraid; those that suspected something was not right didn't care enough about Luke to investigate. While Luke's thoughts darted back and forth, Paul returned. "He took your bonds off," said Luke quietly, "does he fear your prophecy?" Paul moved to sit next to Luke on the floor at the back of the boat.

"I don't think so," Paul said with a sigh, "I think he took them off because we're becoming friends. But I don't think he believes we are in any danger. I tried one last time to get him to turn us around; this time I didn't talk about the vision, I tried to reason with him. I know enough about sailing to know that we shouldn't risk the sea this late in the fall, but he trusts the captain." Paul paused and turned his head to look at Luke, "how you holdin' up?"

"I'm doing alright," Luke said unconvincingly.

Paul chirped up quickly, "Don't worry doctor, I don't think the Lord will let me die before I get to Rome. I think we are safe at least until I get there."

After a long pause Luke spoke up again, "I don't understand why we are going to Rome, if I'm honest. Everyone says that there is nothing but pain and probably death for you there. Why are we doing this?"

Paul had his arms on his knees and was looking down at the ship, "Because God has shown me that I must go and that is good enough for me." There was another long pause.

"It must be nice," Luke said with a smile, "hearing from God directly, always knowing exactly what He wants from you."

Paul smiled, "I don't always know exactly what He wants from me."

"You know what I mean," grinned Luke, "You saw Him face to face. You have seen more miracles and visions than everyone else I know combined; you're not guessing like the rest of us. Or at least nearly as much as the rest of us."

There was another pause. Luke's hair was filled with the gentle western breeze. He looked through the railing at the foaming waves. His travels with Paul made seafaring less enjoyable than it had been, and his anxiety still hung over him. But he still loved the sounds of sea voyages: The boat gently cutting through the water, the soft pat of men's shoes upon the deck, the occasional loud orders, the rhythmic creaks of rope and wood. Each pause was filled with some or all these sounds, making Luke less eager to fill the air with words. After a few minutes Paul broke the seafaring silence, "You're right, I am in a special position. But there is a sense in which I am doing more guessing than you."

Luke furrowed his brow, "In what sense?"

Paul looked at Luke and spread his arms, "Take this ship. I know what doom awaits us, but I can't stop it. I know what God has revealed to me, but I can't on my own make it useful. I have seen many things, but I am often at a loss as to how to communicate them. I am constantly trying to explain things I don't even fully understand and can rarely prove. Yes, I too am often guessing."

Luke, now thoroughly distracted from his fear, quickly responded, "That's not what I mean."

"What do you mean?" Paul retorted.

Luke looked about as if looking for words. "What I mean is this: we know that God wants you to get to Rome. we also know, because God has told you, that if we try to get to Rome quickly, we are in danger. So, why doesn't He just reveal Himself to our captain like he did to you when you were on the road to Damascus? If God really wants us to complete our mission, why doesn't He just show up and explain Himself? That's what I mean. The rest of us are always guessing what God wants, we are hoping and believing that God is near and helping us. But you saw the real thing, you don't have to trust like the rest of us do."

When Luke said this, a tall man interrupted them and asked to speak with Paul privately. Paul told Luke that he would be right back and went to talk to the large, bearded sailor. While they spoke, Luke drank some water and watched the green and blue waves move along the boat. It truly was a beautiful day. When Paul returned, Luke could tell that Paul was in a preaching mood. "Luke, let me explain something to you." Luke sat back against the boat again and got ready to listen.

Paul sat across from Luke and began softly and sternly. "I do not know why God chooses some and not others. I have theories, but I cannot say that I know why. The reality of Adam's sin permeates humanity. The devil opposes us. And the principalities that we create are the easiest thing for Satan to manipulate against us. We cannot be trusted confidants. Even Israel, who God trusted, failed Him. God, in the end, had to become Israel, so that Israel might succeed. God's designs cannot be thwarted, but whether we are chosen or not, we are not safe. In fact, as I search the Scriptures and my own memories, I believe I have identified a general rule in the moral universe, 'the higher, the more in danger.' The average man who is sometimes unfaithful to his wife, sometimes drunk, always a little selfish, now and then (though not unlawfully) dishonest in business, is certainly, by human standards, a lower sort of man. But the harm he might do in the world is small and contained. He may harm his neighbors, but praise be to God, only his neighbors.

"But the type of man I grew up around -The Pharisee, the man of state, the prophet, in short, the man whose soul is filled with some great Cause, to which he will subordinate all things, this is the type of man the enemy can make into a fiend. A man like myself. It seems that when God elevates any man in any way from his peers there is a risk. It is the people God chose who nailed Him to a cross. It is the men born into high standing that are persecuting the Church now. Some are chosen for high spiritual office, others chosen for high political office, but, as we speak, the majority of both these types of men are working against the Lord. Therefore, it seems to me that God must be careful in how much He reveals Himself to Humans. When Christ returns, we will see face to face, but until then we can only be trusted to see shaded reflections.

"But you will say, why does God reveal Himself to anyone? Why does He reveal Himself to some and not others? I must confess again that I do not know, but I will tell you my thoughts. First, because our salvation depends on it. As Isaiah has said, 'As the heavens are higher than the earth, so are my ways higher than your ways and my thoughts than your thoughts.' We have no means by which to reach Him. He is the rock that is higher than I. He must reach down to us, for we cannot climb up to Him. But as the Psalmist says, 'For as high as the heavens are above the earth, so great is His love for those who fear him.' And so, He does reach down to us, for the Love of His people."

Luke was usually very patient when Paul began to preach, but his heart was burning for an answer to his question, and he could not help but feel that Paul was about to go on a tangent and so he interrupted his teacher.

"Paul, please excuse the interruption, but my heart is burning with a different question. You are and have been my teacher as long as I have known you, so please do not be angry with me. For I want you to teach me something specific. I have faith but I seek understanding. Will you allow this interruption?"

Paul looked at Luke smiling and said, "Of course."

Luke was relieved and began his question, "We know that God loves us, for Christ has proved this upon the cross. And we know that God's desire is that the message of reconciliation would reach the entire world, for that is why we are on this journey. But if this is God's desire, why does He not do this Himself? Why not appear to all of us as He did to you? And if it's best not to reveal Himself to everyone there must be some kind of criteria He uses? I guess, what I really want to know is, why hasn't He revealed Himself to me?"

Paul responded, "Is your question fully posed?"

"Yes," Luke said after some delay, "I have thought this for some time and it feels good to ask you, I don't want to sound unfaithful, I just would like to know; if it can be known." Luke felt slightly embarrassed for some indiscernible reason. Part of him felt he had somehow let his teacher down. He looked down to avoid Paul's eyes. The other part of him desperately wanted Paul to have an answer, he had long feared that there was none. He looked back up at Paul hoping for some comfort. He got none.

Paul looked at Luke with an unwavering expression and said, "Will you believe even if there is no answer? If God is silent, will that be enough for you?"

Luke regretted asking his question. At least before he didn't know if there was an answer. After some disappointed hesitation, Luke gathered himself and said, "Yes, even if God does not explain Himself, I can trust that He has an explanation."

Paul smiled, and then said, "Alright, then I will share my thoughts with you." Luke's eyes brightened. The doctor leaned forward once again, ready and excited to hear the old teacher speak.

"As I have already said, mankind is not trustworthy. Thus, God will need to be careful in how He reveals Himself to us. You have asked for criteria, and that I cannot give; because if such a thing does exist, I do not know it. But as I search the Scriptures and look at my own apostleship, some insights present themselves. We know that faith is not like man's wisdom. All men speak beyond what they have experienced and so in some sense all men have faith in things beyond themselves. But this is not the virtue of faith. This is not what the Spirit of God provides. The virtue of faith is personal. I have seen the Isle of Britannia on a map and though I have never been there, I believe that it exists. This is faith, but not the virtue of faith. The virtue of faith is more like believing in a promise that someone has made. It is like acting as if a promise has been and is being kept though you cannot prove it is so. Thus, as our brother

James once told me, there is no faith without faithfulness. This is the virtue of faith, and it is something that each of us must grow in. It is part of our development. God will never put anyone in a position where they are not tasked with bearing the fruit of the Spirit. Therefore, God will never put anyone in a position to not need faith. He will ensure that whatever our circumstances some measure of faith, the virtue of faith, will be tested in us. For in fact, no one can please God apart from faith. I wrote a letter to the Corinthian church where I spoke of the three greatest virtues, and faith was among them.

"Now, why is faith so important? Well I think for the same reason it is important in human relationships, because it enhances love. You and I have shared many adventures together. When I appeared before Agrippa, almost no one came with me for fear of the Jews, but you came, Luke. You told me that you would see my voyage through to the end and be my companion; and you have kept your promise. Would anyone say that we loved each other more when we first met? No! Our love was shallow then. But we have trusted each other, you and I. Has this trust not been the very manifestation of our love? The only way to swim from shallow love into deep love is to trust and trust more. To dive headlong into waters you can't swim alone, hoping that the one you trust will not abandon you. They will carry you and you them in those waters. Every deep friendship, every strong marriage, every bond between child and parent grew into love from the roots of trust and trustworthiness.

This is the nature of personal relationships, and there can be no other way.

"And so, if our relationship with God is going to mean anything, it will grow from the same roots. We will have to learn to trust God *and* become trustworthy. He will have to set us on journeys that seem impossible apart from Him. He will have to place us in labyrinths only He has escaped. We will face riddles so complex with answers so complicated that we cannot even attend to it; and we will be asked to trust the small pieces we can know. We will, in most respects, find ourselves in the position of children. Neither understanding what the grownups say nor understanding why they say it. For children learn numbers and letters for reasons they cannot understand, in order that they may one day perform tasks that, as children, sound boring to them in order to take on responsibilities that, as children, they certainly do not want and could not even imagine wanting. For what little boy, who hates cleaning his room, would rejoice at being told to clean and care for the entire house? But we know that the child once grown up, should he get his own home will rejoice in it. What little girl learning her sums would be overjoyed when asked to balance a budget? But we know the joy this same girl will feel when she, for the first time, goes to market, with her own money, carefully accounted for, to purchase clothes or food. And so, my dear Luke, since we are but infants to God, let us rejoice in our status, for as our Lord has said of children, 'The kingdom of heaven belongs to such as these.'"

Paul and Luke

One classic feature of Paul's preaching would be his breaking out into fits of praise to Jesus. Luke could often see such fits coming. Whenever Paul felt he had sufficiently described the mysteries of God as they had been revealed in Christ, Paul would begin quoting his favorite psalms or hymns to God. Paul loved to sing, and Luke could feel a song coming over his friend. However, on this occasion, Paul was interrupted. A group of men came to throw some waste overboard and told Paul and Luke to move aside. Upon finishing their task, the men walked away, all except one. He stayed behind, waiting until the men had passed out of ear shot. He then came meekly to Paul. He took Paul aside and they spoke together a moment. Paul then prayed for him and the man went in the direction of the other men.

"What was that about?" Luke asked, half not wanting to know so that Paul could get back to what he was saying.

"The man said he was also nervous about setting sail this late in the fall and he wanted to know how certain I was that we would crash. I told him I was certain. He then asked if I would ask my God to protect Him. I began to share with Him the Gospel of Christ, but he said he needed to get back to the others and asked if I would quickly pray. I told Him I cannot guarantee his protection but that I would pray."

Such scenes were not uncommon to Paul, but Luke was always impressed. Paul had such a one-track mind. His fervor and commitment gave him the countenance of a sage among men. He was not like the rest of us. As Luke was thinking these things about his friend, he noticed Paul had stopped talking and looked like he was confused.

"Is everything alright?" Luke asked.

"Well, my son," Paul said with an embarrassed smile, "I am an old man, and I'm afraid I cannot remember what we were talking about."

Luke laughed and then worked to rekindle his teacher's memory, "You had restated that mankind is sinful and therefore unreliable. We may do more harm than good if God entrusts mankind with his revelation indiscriminately. Not only this, God desires to have strong, loving and meaningful relationships with us, meaning He must place us in situations where we can trust Him and prove ourselves trustworthy. Or to use words you've often said to me, that 'faith may be credited to us as righteousness.' And the last thing you said was that this will put us in the position of children. Which to me makes sense because God's age and wisdom obviously dwarfs our own and since…"

"Yes, yes" Paul interrupted, "thank you Luke, do you mind if I pick up from here?"

"Not at all," said Luke, happy to see Paul's wits about him again.

"Very good, thank you. All that you have said is true, but you may ask of me, 'has the burden of faith been lifted from you, my father? Has God not revealed Himself to you and asked you to live not by faith but by sight?' To answer this, I again take us to the example of Israel. Our ancestors have, at times, believed that Israel was selected out of some hatred for all other nations and a special favoritism for Israel. But that is not what God said to our forefather Abraham. 'All peoples on earth will be blessed through you.' In other words, the chosen people are not chosen for their own sake but for the sake of the unchosen. Has it ever puzzled you, now having read the Scriptures, why our people are called the Israelites and not the Abrahamites or the Iassacites or even the Jacobites? We are called Israel for precisely the reason Jacob was called Israel: We are a people who will struggle with God and men and prevail. We are a people chosen not for special pleasure or even honor, but for a special burden. We are born for a special struggle. We are chosen to suffer. Our sufferings are great, but as Isaiah foresaw, our sufferings heal others.

"Both Messiah and Christ mean Anointed or chosen one. If what I have said is true, is it any surprise that the truest son of Israel, the Messiah, the Christ, would heal all men by His suffering? That through His faith in His Father, He might fulfill the destiny of Israel? There seems to be a principle of vicariousness in nature. A child survives upon its mother. We survive upon the earth. Life on earth survives upon the sun and many other things. It seems that the ones chosen for special tasks, the ones who receive the special visions, the men and women selected to special intimacy are also selected for special suffering. They are the ones upon whom their brothers and sisters will depend. Their life and resources will be used up for the sake of others. Has this not been true of me?

"I have been beaten with whips, with rods, with stones. I face danger from Gentiles, I face danger from Jews. I have been hungry and thirsty, tired and alone. I have been sick and I have been afraid. In short, I have been put in unique positions to trust Christ. He who is blessed forever, chose me and revealed Himself to me, not that I may avoid learning faith but that my faith may be tested more extremely. For, make no mistake, I have been confused. The Lord's plan for me, to this very hour, seems to work only towards my harm.

"I have been told by the Spirit that all things are working together for my good, but apart from hourly fixing my mind upon the resurrection, I cannot see how this is true; for my daily experience is in the main suffering. Even within the Church I am hated and persecuted. If for this life I live I am among the most foolish and pitiable men who have existed. Every day my faith is tested because every day I am tempted to quit; to disbelieve the vision that has, humanly speaking torn my life apart. I was respected and in high standing, now I am a prisoner. I was the persecutor, now I am the persecuted. When I sacrifice, I am asked to sacrifice more. Often the words of Jeremiah tug upon my mind, 'You deceived me, Lord, and I was deceived; you overpowered me and prevailed. I am ridiculed all day long; everyone mocks me.'

"But then I am reminded to shield myself in *faith*. For the Lord sees farther than I. He sees the end result of my offering to Him; the final fruit of my labor. He sees the

Last Day when we will be glorified together, He in me and I in Him. And beyond that, I know that it is only through faith that I can become what I was intended to be. It is only through faith that Christ can live in me. What if, my dear Luke, God has died for me, believing that I would die for Him? Would it not be an honor when I finally see Him again to tell Him that *His* faith was not in vain? Humanity cannot be trusted, but perhaps some chosen few can. God chose David and not His brothers because of some unseen thing in David's heart. Might this always be the case? Perhaps, there are men whose heart's He trusts? I would like to be one of those. To be so surrendered to the power and will of God, that I, like Job, did not let Him down. Yes, indeed, I hope that is why I am alive.

"But that is for me. For many others God will simply ask that they trust and not see. My belief is that they will be spared great pain. If Abraham was chosen to be a blessing, those that were unchosen for the task were chosen to receive that blessing. Perhaps, one day, generations yet unborn will read about my life and worship our Lord Jesus Christ because of me. And so, the blessing of Abraham's seed will, in some small way, flow by God's grace through me."

Paul paused for a moment; his eyes had welled up with tears. Luke, wanting to help his teacher, interjected, "If I have my way, the Church at the very least will not forget what God has done in you." As the tears began to fall down Paul's face he smiled and spoke to Luke.

"May Christ be glorified." After saying this Paul's expression changed and became almost severe. "Luke, God reveals Himself to whom He wishes. But I hope you have heard me well. It seems to me quite likely that God does not reveal Himself to the many because He seeks to bless them. He wants faith from them and the more He reveals of Himself the more extravagant and difficult the trials must be for them. I have seen the risen Lord and so the rest of my life has been a demonstration that I trust God in other ways. That I trust in His plans even though they seem impossible and often in conflict with my personal good. But to those whom He reveals less, less trials are required for their faith. We all have been created to do good works which He prepared in advance for us to do. We live in a world stained by sin, where suffering must come. But it is not God's will for us to suffer. He does not delight in evil. And so, I believe that God tempers His revelation to the many that He might keep them from the bitter cup. That He might spare them the wrath of the world, the flesh and the devil. For all three torture and destroy anyone that they fear threatens them. All of us must face them to some degree, but that degree will be in perfect proportion to the grace God reveals to each person. And so, my dear Luke, I do not believe it a mere flattery, those words our Lord said to our brother Thomas the night He appeared to him, 'blessed are those who have not seen me and yet believe'."

Afterword

The Illustrated London News, Issue #7,044
The Strong and Satisfied God
By: Mr. Clive Gilbert Lewis Keith esquire

Some months ago, God in the flesh gave a speech to the Oxford Union. I believe that it is safe to say that this speech is the most important event of my lifetime. It is an event that has reshaped the world. The religion of this space-man-God has exploded into every nook and cranny of the earth. He is being hailed as a liberator in the streets and a messiah from the rooftops. People study His teaching night and day and are hourly translating His speech into the lesser spoken languages. The ramifications of His remarks are felt across the globe politically, socially, economically, philosophically, and even gastronomically. At this very hour, I am eating a popsicle ice cream bar in the shape of God's spaceship, as well as a slice of a cake replicating His podium. Momentous. Thanks be to God. I have enjoyed the parades through the streets to worship this space-man-God, and I am enjoying eating this popsicle. But I would be remiss not to mention some of my difficulties with Him and perhaps give pause for some, who have immediately seen Him as a messiah before examining His merits as a God.

Before I go any further, I feel I must confess an unfair disposition that I have against space-man-God, and that is this: His horrendous use of the English language. I do not dare give omniscience any advice, which is why this is a confession and not a critique. I did not like the use of language by space-man-God or the brevity of His usage. Given how infrequently space-man-God visits us, I would have loved more content. But I recognize that this is not my place. To make such demands upon space-man-God, should he be the creator, is out-of-court and evil. I repent. Having now openly confessed my natural, yet sinful, predisposition I can move to examine what kind of Deity, space-man-God has revealed himself to be.

Despite saying very few words, space-man-God managed to communicate even less than he said. From His nine and one-half-page speech, I can decipher only two actual doctrines from this God.

The first is that he is not a pantheistic God. In other words, he does not animate the universe as you would animate your body. The universe is not God. This doctrine can be understood based on two of space-man-God's assertions. First, He (God) had a message to communicate to us (presumably not God). If this God were pantheistic, then the way that we would come to a knowledge of Him would be through better understanding ourselves. It would be through some mystical process of journeying inward that we would discover the God within. But this is not what space-man-God had us do. The second piece of evidence that discourages a pantheistic view of space-man-God is His moral teaching. If you do not distinguish between good and bad very seriously, then it is easy to say that anything you find in this world is a part of God. But, of course, if you think some things are actually wrong and God actually good, then you cannot place your faith in pantheism. You must believe that God is separate from the world and that some things we see in it are contrary to his will. Confronted with cancer or racism, the pantheist can say, 'If you could only see it from the divine point of view, you would realize that this also is God.' But this is not what space-man-God revealed.

My intuition has always agreed with the first of space-man-God's doctrines, that God is not pantheistic. Of the half-dozen pantheistic schemes I have read, they all have a fantastic and inexplicable center of gravity. For in pantheism, the universe is not something that God created. It is a secretion—it comes out of Him. Or the universe is only an illusion, it is something He looks like to us but really is not. Pantheism is even sometimes described as a universe unaccountably suffering from a severe and possibly permanent case of schizophrenia. In addition to the "out of the blue" nature of pantheism, its implications for humanity seem, at least to me, wildly counterintuitive.

For the pantheist, everything is really *one* thing. This is hard to reconcile with one's experience. There appears to be a wonderful external world in which I live. The world seems filled with things that existed before I did and things that will exist when I am gone. But pantheism removes the astonishing things. Because there is really only one thing: the universe, which is impersonal and cannot be astonished at anything. But an even stranger implication is what I already mentioned about morality. There is no real possibility of getting out of pantheism any particular impulse to moral action. For pantheism implies that one thing is as good as another, whereas action implies in its nature that one thing is vastly preferable to another. And all moral teaching accepts as an axiom that particular behavior is, by its nature, preferable to other behavior.

And so, with space-man-God and his billions of newly converted followers, I find myself in rousing agreement. For a God with only two doctrines, I am happy to say that we agree on 50% of them. But, now I come to His second doctrine. A doctrine as puzzling as the moral teaching that flows naturally from it. And that is the doctrine that the powerful are to be trusted. This, to me, is a particularly damning doctrine, and it is why I cannot, in good conscience, affirm the deity of this spaceman.

Afterword

One might think that the most definitive proof for "Original Sin," or what might be more accurately called the 'Fall of Man,' lay in the colossal human failures of war, famine, disease, sexual immorality, drugs, theft, gossip, malice, and the like. But I think that the far more definitive proof for the Fall of Man lay not in emphasizing his failure but shining a clear light on his success. For if humanity's greatness is mired in weakness, what argument is left against the doctrine of the Fall?

There are few dispositions more self-annihilating than the worship of success. What I mean is not that if a person worships success, they will be annihilated. Instead, I mean that the disposition of worshiping success will kill itself. For every man, however wise, who begins by honoring success, will end in glorifying mediocrity. I am not saying that men are too weak to worship success and achieve it; I am saying that the worship of success is too weak to achieve it.

The paradox is inherent in the belief. This is easily understood when we consider the most successful and heroic men of history. Augustus Caesar, the mightiest of the Caesars, became such not by accomplishing only those tasks that he thought he could reasonably achieve, but rather by accomplishing tasks that got more excellent warriors killed. He did not achieve more greatness than his uncle Julius by carefully pursuing only those endeavors of which success was certain. Nay, he lived his life as close to failure as he could reasonably manage. When Octavian challenged giants like Lepidus and Antony he did not do this because the outcome was 'in the bag.' Those lions, Antony in particular, would have been the favorite out the gate. The man who would become Augustus Caesar risked his life every day while he was Octavian. His attitude was to achieve greatness or die trying. He welcomed failure to his door nightly that he might visibly, covered in blood, deny it entry. And his call to all the hounds of doom rang out not to ensure success, but, if he survived, ensure something else: glory. He risked his life to prove that he genuinely was first among equals; that among the proud men of Rome, none deserved Rome more than he. And he would kill or be killed in this quest. He profaned the natural pathways of success and became more successful. This is the tale of all great men, of all heroes, good and evil.

They achieve greatness not by running away from risk but by running into it. A man may become a hero for the sake of his country, like Scipio. He may equally become a hero for the sake of his philosophy, like Socrates, but not for the sake of success. Obviously, a man may choose to risk failure because he loves his country or philosophy; but he cannot risk failure because he loves success.

Our relationship to success is one of the many paradoxes we bear. We are forbidden to worship success, yet we must strive to achieve it if we are to strive at all. This paradox in the nature of things unravels the mystery of why all human power is un-maintainable. The moment we become successful, we want to remain so. The moment success is the standard; risk becomes increasingly unendurable. But

Afterword

if risk cannot be suffered, then the only achievements the strong man can strive for are those that do not strain his strength. And suddenly, all pathways to improvement wane. This is the loss of what the Americans call, "the eye of the Tiger." And so, humanity comes at the last, to a sort of tedium and acquiescence. We worship success, or another way of saying it, we worship strength. But to worship strength is simply to worship the *status quo,* for strength is the keeper of the status quo. Goliath fights men he is certain to kill and the Philistines become weak in their dependence upon him. But David, the truly strong man, fights men who are almost certain to beat him and Israel enters its golden age under him. The truly strong man is courageous. He, by his courage, risks failure and challenges the strong, that he may become stronger than they. As any powerlifter will tell you, you will not get stronger if you are not straining your muscles to the point of tearing them apart. But if success is worshiped, no such risk can be taken. This is the process by which almost every great civilization has died. It killed the Babylonians and the Persians, the Carthaginians and Romans, those the Chinese conquered, and the Chinese themselves and so many others.

This doom that lays over humanity is the tragic irony of our existence. This is the great proof of the Fall of man. This is the doom that swirls about even the best of human plans and institutions, and it infallibly demonstrates the fallibility of us all. Like waves of the sea, we rise, we crest, and, with fury, come down to nothing. Each civilization hopes to be different. Each civilization desires permanence. But each civilization has failed. As chronic and predictable as this doom has been, so also is the process by which it has come about. That process stated succinctly is this; the very thing which makes a civilization great, eventually works against that very greatness. We are a race doomed to forever endanger ourselves by protecting ourselves. It is mankind's desire for sustained success that produces each collapse. And this process is in full swing in our day, and the spaceman has given the powerful all they need to enact a more complete collapse than ever before.

It is for the maintenance of success that humans create processes, create formulas. Creating formulas, like pursuing success, is good and natural. But like success, makes a terrible God. In our modern economy, the recipe most tightly connected with power and wealth is that of marketing or propaganda. Every business, leader, and idealist pursues and creates propaganda machines to maintain their sales, abilities, and movements, respectively. They work to shoot their propaganda further. It is wider messaging that makes a broader audience. It is a more general audience that creates a wider consumer base. This propagandizing formula is simple and effective. But it bears a weakness, one that is plain to anyone that has ever been duped by it; good marketing has no relationship to truth or goodness. Something might be popular that does not make it morally upright. Something may be believed widely—that does not mean it is true.

Afterword

A thing may have all of the propagandists of the earth fashioning songs declaring it's worthiness, and yet, be unworthy. From this vantage point, one can consider humanity's perilous situation. Consider this: The more successful your civilization, the wider you may market yourself. The wider you're dealing, the further the distance between the ears hearing the propaganda and the things propagandized. The further that distance, the harder to disprove the propaganda. For they cannot test whether you are lying. They cannot say this thing doesn't work, for they have never seen the thing. They either fight against the influential people who tell them what to think or believe what they are told. The people with the most extensive propaganda machines will be the most powerful in this world. If the old maxim is true, that power tends to corrode character, only one conclusion naturally follows. The ones most likely to tell a lie will be the same ones who most benefit from, and quickly can, tell a lie.

We create processes to ensure success, and in our modern world, the most common approach is that of propaganda. But none of these processes, least of all propaganda, will ensure that what we advertise and encourage is good, beautiful, or even beneficial.

Upon such a world, a "God" in a flying machine descended some months ago. He came bearing advice. Advice he entrusted to the most powerful, wealthy, and well-known people on our planet. He came, entrusting Himself to the propagandists. The shapers of processes. The seekers of formulas. And if there be anyone on earth who worships the status quo, it is the people the spaceman came and made His apostles. He is the celebrity God, commercialized and dramatized in all the trappings of royalty and fanfare of Hollywood. But if this is God, if this is indeed our creator, does this seem fitting at all? How can simply participating in our brokenness heal us? If the way we use and see power is flawed, and if even our success can divorce itself from truth and goodness, then why come using our existing power systems? How can such a God possibly broker change by further entrenching man in the modes of power that already fail Him?

Two thousand years ago, according to Christianity, a different Godman came. And he came not in a spaceship or palace. He came in poverty and anonymity. He came proclaiming that, "The kings of the Gentiles exercise lordship over them, and those in authority over them are called benefactors. But not so with you. Rather, let the greatest among you become as the youngest and the leader as one who serves." But our messiah came and made demands. He came and was served. He came and acted like any other head of state and unsurprisingly recruited such men to hear and preach His message. A message which is essentially, "I am here for the wealthy, that they may marvel and gawk at me and then I am leaving; They can handle it from there." Is this the type of salvation humanity needs?

Atrocities are experienced everyday by ordinary people. I can, with almost utter certainty, say that a murder, a rape, an illness, a theft, an accident, an abduction, a loss, a burglary, and probably dozens of other such evils have happened today. This is undoubtedly serious and ought to take us to our knees day and night. But I can, with almost utter certainty, also say that a birthday, a worship service, an act of sharing, a kiss of love, a warm embrace, a hearty family meal, a joke amongst friends, a hope fulfilled also happened today. This is the precarious position wherein mankind finds itself. Under peaceful and free conditions, good and evil will befall our race and nothing in this world will remedy it. Pain and happiness will apply itself liberally and often, randomly. These are the plagues and pleasures of mankind. But the plagues end in death for all men, while the pleasures, but for faith, do not end in eternal and joyful life. Thus, the plagues loom large over mankind. These universal plagues are those things that both common and powerful men alike try to avoid or control; and it cannot but serve as a regular testimony to our weakness; a weakness of shame or sadness or both. But when history is made, as it so often is, by the sword, the situation changes. While the mighty man and common man see the plagues as equals, the mighty man and the common man see the sword differently. If indeed the mighty man is mighty he is the blade's wielder. While the best the common man might hope for is to be neglected by or become a powerful sword —for he has no means to wield it. The mighty man drafts men into his army. The common man either finds himself avoiding the draft or praying that he survives the war he has been drafted into. The sword is a different type of plague.

But history not only speaks of wars, those uses of the sword against the outer adversary, but also persecutions, those ages when the powerful turn the sword inward. During the persecutions, the experience of the common and the mighty man is in the most juxtaposition. When the blade turns inward, the most powerful men turn the sword thus. The most powerful men feel most in control. They have never been safer, and their enemies never more in peril. But the common man never feels less in control. Whether he avoids the sword or not, or even if he is the sword, slashing against the chest of his brothers, no ordinary man feels safe or in control. For the common man trusted in the armies of his leaders to protect him. The men who now bring him harm are the same ones who made him safe. The common men serve the mighty men against other common men and feel as helpless as those they slay. Thus, we hear stories of Nazis who showed kindness to Jews in the concentration camps, but who didn't feel up to the challenge of actually saving their lives. No, they forced them into the gas chambers, same as those Nazis who hated them. One feels shame and the other satisfaction, but they both force them in. This is the plight of the common man in such times; even if he finds the persecution unjustified, he feels powerless to do anything about it.

These are the great atrocities of history. In the wake of such moments, words like tyrant, despot, dictator, autocrat, bully, oppressor, slaver, and dozens more are invented. The greatest villains of history are not those that sacked the cities of neighboring nations, though many of them were villains. The greatest villains are they that burnt the homes, raped the women, killed the children, and slowly tortured the men who, by nationality, ought to have been their friends. They are the spiritual children of Cain, killing their younger brothers.

I apologize for how long it has taken me to get to my point. No doubt I seem like a rambling old man, and I probably am. But now I have come to the end. Throughout history, there have been local justifications to turn the sword inward. Always in different places and at different times, but there has never been a justification for all the most powerful, in every area and at the same time to purge the unfaithful, until now. This spaceman has given it to them. The most powerful in our world have the endorsement of God to dictate to others with clear consciences. He has given them his words. He selected them from all the peoples of the earth. Without changing their visions, he has stoked their aspirations and sanctified their leadership. They are the chosen. Like the apostles of Christ, they are the sent ones to go out into the world and be his witnesses. Like the prophets of old, they are His mouthpieces. Any internal tug of conscience the powerful may have had against their control, no longer has any basis. Any outcry from the weak can now be dismissed. Any intellectual defiance a politician may have concocted must now be put aside, for God has spoken; the new creation must begin. If there ever was a justification for turning the sword inward, it is the justification of this spaceman. The powerful were chosen; they must now use their power.

Christ took the opposite course, and it was the paradox of His power that led me weeping and joyful to Him. He used the weak things of this world to shame the strong. The foolish things to shame the wise. With all the wisdom of eternity, the most omnipotent being became a poor boy from a small village. This was the only hope for the virtue of humility. Unless God could find a way to humiliate Himself, no being would be justified in doing it. Pride, not humility, would have been the pathway to salvation. The pagans already thought it was, with all the good sense in the world. He came as a helpless baby. He was weaned, in all likelihood, by a teenage mother perhaps no more than a hundred pounds. But God went further to demonstrate His humility. He died, for beings as little worthy of it as could be imagined. He did not die for angels who had served Him faithfully. But for humans who were making their natures a contradiction to His—spoiling His world in the process. He abased Himself in *death*, the state most opposite to Himself, that they might live. And in humility defeated His opposite. But His humiliation goes still further. In the Scriptures, when a demon possesses a man, it forces him by torture to do the demon's will. But the Spirit of God does not do this. Even if we want Him to; believe me, I have asked. No, the Spirit of God is a helper. He will not correct the will by breaking it, He will only correct the will by empowering it. He will obey and encourage the few good desires of those who receive Him. He uses His power to empower, nothing more. This is humility through and through.

For the promotion of humility, the God of the Bible begins His stories not with proclamations but with demonstrations. Abraham is taken on a journey before his descendants receive a law. The ten commandments themselves begin, not with a commandment but a reminder of Israel and Yahweh's shared history. "I am the Lord your God, who brought you out of the land of Egypt, out of the house of slavery." David is given promises, and God fulfills them, and only then is he commanded to build a temple. And Jesus says, "Follow me," years before He says, "Abide in me." The God of the Bible begins by saying, "Let me show you that I am good," before He ever commands, "Be good."

And this brings me to my final and most pronounced objection to the spaceman who calls Himself God. This tall, handsome, polite man introduced to us as the Almighty has said many flattering things about Himself and about us. But has he proved them? He has said that he is good. But to whom has he shown His goodness? He has said that he loves us, but what does he mean by this phrase? Some people say they love their families, and others love their food; how is "God" using this word when he says it to us? He comes to us and speaks words we say to each other every day. He recites Facebook posts my niece might have written. He says all the familiar things a television host might repeat about God, and, without another word or action, he sends the world a peace sign and peaces out. What does this man mean?

Some may think that I am joining the small chorus of objectors who are both confused and offended by God's pathetic use of the English language. I am not. Some may think I hate that His style has been embraced at the popular level. On the contrary, it is one of the few things about this deity that I find appealing. Some may think I am frustrated with giant swathes of humanity leaving Christianity in order to follow the "True God's Religion." This is regrettable; however, this is not my issue with Him. My problem, lest anyone is confused, is that this "God" came to humanity speaking of His goodness, speaking of His love, speaking of endless joy and hope for tomorrow. And then he does nothing. I do not deny the existence of goodness, but what assurances do I have that this large man is the source of that goodness? What goodness did he, in the 22 hours that we knew Him, display?

In short, what I am arguing is that a man's worth is not dependent on what he *says* about His moral conduct; it is dependent *on* His moral conduct. We have heard from "God" that he is good. But goodness is not in the telling; it is in the doing. In other words, the claim of merit can only be confirmed or denied through history. The God of the Old Testament spoke of His goodness and then did good things among Israel, and then in the New Testament, He did one better. He became an ordinary man and showed men not

Afterword

just that He was good but how they might imitate His goodness. It is the moral life of Jesus that drew men and women to Him. But the "God" of our age asks for genuinely blind faith. When men say that talk is cheap, they are actually underselling it. Nay my friends, by itself, talk is worthless.

www.ingramcontent.com/pod-product-compliance
Lightning Source LLC
Chambersburg PA
CBHW071130020225
21281CB00016B/1649